"That's nice," Dimitri said absently, crossing the room to where she was.

"There is something else I've been thinking about. Something else I think I would enjoy immensely."

Then he pulled her to him and kissed her. But "he kissed her" was a little like saying "he dropped the bomb and it went off." It felt like more, much more. His arms were around her with possessive, almost bruising strength, his mouth was on hers, his tongue parting her lips (which, to be fair, were open in surprise, so it wasn't exactly difficult), and he was pulling her against him so she was standing on tiptoe. And kissing him back, of course. Why not? It was the chance of a lifetime.

Caitlyn brought her hands up and put them on his broad chest, warm even through his T-shirt. Her tongue touched his and she bit his lower lip lightly, and he made a sound, some sound, and tightened his grip.

"Well?" she gasped, pulling back. "Were you right? Did you enjoy it immensely?"

"I did."

HELLO, GORGEOUS!

MaryJanice Davidson

KENSINGTON BOOKS
http://www.kensingtonbooks.com

KENSINGTON BOOKS are published by

Kensington Publishing Corp.
850 Third Avenue
New York, NY 10022

All Kensington titles, imprints and distributed lines are available at special quantity discounts for bulk purchases for sales promotion, premiums, fund-raising, educational or institutional use.

Special book excerpts or customized printings can also be created to fit specific needs. For details, write or phone the office of the Kensington Special Sales Manager: Kensington Publishing Corp., 850 Third Avenue, New York, NY 10022. Attn. Special Sales Department. Phone: 1-800-221-2647.

ISBN-13: 978-0-7582-0805-7
ISBN-10: 0-7582-0805-7

First Trade Paperback Printing: March 2005
First Mass Market Paperback Printing: May 2007
10 9 8 7 6 5 4 3 2 1

Printed in the United States of America

This book is not for Scott Gottlieb.

Acknowledgments

Once again, I'm shocked to find out I don't write these books by myself. Friends and family are mentioned on my acknowledgments page in lieu of royalties.

As always, thanks to my husband, Anthony, for tirelessly reading and listening and reading some more, usually with that dratted purple pen in one hand. He not only reads rough drafts, he comes up with story ideas! I'd better check and see if Minnesota is a community property state. . . .

Thanks also to my sister, Yvonne, for always giving me the straight poop (I will call a girlfriend to hear what I want to hear, but I will call my sister for the truth), and also to Denise and Crystal, who always buy my books and do a credible imitation of liking them as well.

Thanks also to Cathleen, for thinking up Mother-in-law Jeopardy.

Extra-special thanks to the world's greatest proofreader, Karen Thompson, and all the gang over at Loose-ID Publications (www.loose-id.com), who are nice enough to pretend not to mind when other writing obligations prevent me from writing another story for them.

Finally, thanks to my editor, Kate Duffy, who was not remotely afraid when I told her my plan for a cybernetic sorority girl.

"The person who designed a robot that could act and think as well as your four-year-old would deserve a Nobel Prize. But there is no public recognition for bringing up truly human beings."
—C. John Sommerville
The Rise and Fall of Childhood

"We can rebuild him. We have the technology."
—*The Six Million Dollar Man*

Prologue

Nine days after she died, Caitlyn James woke up in a private hospital in Minnesota.

This was problematic, because her last memory was of passing out in the backseat of a Miami limo.

It was a private hospital room, in itself a miracle in these days of HMOs and accountants making medical decisions. One such accountant was in the room with her. He was leaning over her bed and moving his lips. He had thinning blond hair, rimless glasses, and was wearing an utterly spotless lab coat. No name tag. No hospital name stitched over his pocket. She dubbed him Egghead #1.

She squinted at #1, and as if someone were turning up the volume in her head, he slowly became audible.

". . . everything's all right. You're in a branch of the O.S.F. in Minneapolis, Minnesota."

"Minnesota?" she rasped. No hangover, that was something. A miraculous something. She was reasonably certain she and her girlfriends had been mixing Kahlúa and tequila. Or had it been tequila and Baileys? They'd been mixing *something* with chocolate milk. . . .

She sure felt like she could spit cotton though. Her mouth was as dry as the desert. She reached for the shiny cup beside her bed, but it crumpled in her hand. Dammit! She'd do anything, *lay* anything, for a glass of water.

"Minnesota?" she tried again, clearing her throat.

"Yes. There were special circumstances and we had to airlift you here."

I. Am. So. Thirsty. "Sorry, I wasn't listening. What?"

"We had to airlift you here and—and there are some things I need to go over with you."

"What day is it?" Rent was due on Monday, and she'd be damned if Old Lady Shea was going to nail her with another fifty-dollar late fee. Like the woman needed more money to bury in her chive patch. "The day . . . what—what time is it?"

"It's October thirty-first. Halloween," Egghead #1 added brightly, as if looking forward to a brisk round of trick-or-treating after work. "Just after lunchtime, in fact. If you're hungry, I could—"

"Hallo—" She cut herself off, shocked. The party had been on the twentieth. Her twenty-fourth birthday. She and a bunch of her sorority sisters had rented a limo and driven from Minneapolis to Miami. Things got a little blurry after her sixth piña colada. They got even blurrier after the Kahlúa-Baileys-chocolate-milk mixture.

Where were her friends? Why was *she* still here? Had there been an accident?

Oh, God . . . *had* there?

She grabbed Egghead #1's lapel, meaning to pull him closer so she could get some answers. Instead, to her surprise (and, doubtless, Egghead's), he sailed right over the top of her bed and crashed into the wall above her, then fell directly on her. For a wonder, there was no pain, just the annoyance of being smothered by a squirming accountant.

Caitlyn sat up, startled, pushed Egghead #1 off her, ignored his groan as he tumbled to the floor, and noticed a curious thing: no IVs. No bandages. No soreness. She wasn't even dizzy. Thirsty, yes. Hurt, no.

So why was she still here? And where *was* here?

Suddenly, shockingly—by far the most startling thing to happen to her so far, and it had been a *weird* five minutes—there was something on her eye.

Target pulse rate: 142. Target blood pressure: 140/120.

Chance of target engaging in deceit: 92.628%

TARGET IS STRESSED REPEAT TARGET IS STRESSED

Correction: there was something in her brain. Something in her brain that thought this fellow on the floor was lying to her . . . or getting ready to.

"Why is there a picture in my head?" Before he could answer, she had another one for him. "What the hell is going on?" She was more puzzled than angry. Anger would come later.

"There are a few other things I have to tell you," #1 groaned from the floor.

Part One

Chapter 1

—Original Message—
From: Donald Carlson, head of O.S.F. Research, Development, and Experimentation
<dcarlson.RDE@osf.link>
To: The Boss <TheBoss@osf.link>
Sent: Monday, September 01, 2004 4:01 PM
Subject: Recent Acquisition

Subject was acquired at 0110 hours today via one of our private ambulances. Subject is a Caucasian female in apparent good health, except for being clinically dead, with an alcohol blood level of .20. Subject is seventy inches tall and weighs one hundred seventy pounds. No birthmarks or apparent scars; however, subject has a tattoo on her lower back in dark blue ink that reads CAVEAT EMPTOR. Subject has shoulder-length dark blue hair (presumably dyed) and light blue eyes (Dr. Miller likens them to the color of the deep end of a swimming pool, but then, he's always been a poetic freak). Subject was in a car accident at 0105 hours with five other females of roughly the same age. Subject got the worst of it because another car hit the side of the limousine in which she was riding. Three of the other five have been released with minor injuries; two have broken bones and are currently recovering at Miami General Hospital.

Subject has no immediate family; parents were killed (irony here, Boss) in a car crash when Subject was thirteen. Subject's last known relative, a paternal aunt, died eighteen months ago.

Basically, Boss, she's legally dead and we can do whatever we like with her.

—Dr. Don

—Original Message—
From: The Boss <TheBoss@osf.link>
To: Dr. Don Carlson
<dcarlson.RDE@osf.link>
Sent: Monday, September 01, 2004 4:11 PM
Subject: Re: Recent Acquisition

Sounds promising. What about her friends?

—Original Message—
From: Donald Carlson, head of O.S.F. Research, Development, and Experimentation
<dcarlson.RDE@osf.link>

To: The Boss <TheBoss@osf.link>
Sent: Monday, September 01, 2004 4:01
PM
Subject: Re: Re: Recent Acquisition

They think she's still in Florida and are un-
likely to discover otherwise—a bunch of former sorority girls. Not exactly the sharpest
knives in the drawer . . . plus, they all went
to a state school. No problems there.
We can tell them she died (which is the
truth, frankly) or we can tell them she's
going to be in the hospital for a few more
weeks or we can tell them she turned into a
bird and flew away.
Come on, Boss. Give me a green light. This
one's perfect.

—Original Message—
From: The Boss <TheBoss@osf.link>
To: Dr. Don Carlson
<dcarlson.RDE@osf.link>
Sent: Monday, September 01, 2004 4:11 PM
Subject: Re: Re: Recent Acquisition

Go. Update me hourly.

Chapter 2

Two months later
St. Paul, Minnesota

"Jimmy! Dude! I heard you were dead!"

Caitlyn set down her daiquiri and looked over her shoulder. *My, my. Look what the cat coughed up.* Her old college roommate, Stacy Gwen, had just walked into the bar. Although Caitlyn normally distrusted people with two first names, she made an exception in Stacy's case.

"For the zillionth time," she said, patting the empty barstool beside her, "don't call me Jimmy." She paused, not sure what else to say. She hadn't seen Stacy since the fateful limo ride in October. "What's up?"

"What's up, she says!"

"Also for the millionth time, it's so disturbing when you talk about people in the third person."

"Oh my God, I totally cannot believe you're here!" Stacy seized her and pulled her into a hug, nearly yanking Caitlyn off her barstool. Surprised, and touched, she hugged her friend back. "So bizarre! You, like, pulled a Houdini after the limo crashed. I mean, we were going crazy! *I* was going crazy! I mean, hello, what is *up* with that?"

Caitlyn settled herself back on the stool, bit into her strawberry garnish, and considered what to say.

Well, Stace old girl, I'll tell you how it was. You'll like this one. Seems that the limo driver had been helping himself to cocaine, which he chased with tequila shots. And the six of us in the back were so blitzed, we didn't notice.

Wait, it gets better. So the moron crashed into the First National Bank of Miami, setting off about a zillion alarms, and, since none of us was wearing seat belts, cracking the shit out of the rest of us. Pretty dumb about the seat belts, I know, so don't start.

Then another car came by and hit my side of the limo, further cracking the shit out of yours truly. I mean, up until then it had been a reasonably cool evening.

Then this lame government service, who'd been watching and listening to police bands all over the country for a month or so, heard and came to the hospital where we were being worked on. And they picked me, because I was the most banged up. And they flew me to their secret government installation. I know how it sounds. I died a couple of times on the way, but they brought me back.

And they made some . . . um . . . changes.

And now I'm supposed to work for them, do you believe that shit? They did things to me and I'm supposed to thank them and become a government employee. Except I don't want to, because I didn't ask for any of this.

And they don't like that. Not at all.

So here I am.

"It's been kind of a weird fall," she said, sad and

mad at the same time—as early as three months ago, she could have told Stacy anything.

Those days were done. *Thanks tons, United States government.*

"Well, are you free?"

"According to some," she said gloomily, "no."

"Uh-huh. Let's go grab some sushi."

"A fine plan," she agreed.

Stacy laughed as Caitlyn hopped off the barstool. "You still slay me, girlfriend. I love the way you talk. You were totally the brains behind Tau Delta Nu."

"A heroic achievement."

Stacy cracked up again. "And don't even pretend like I don't know you're slamming me, Jimmy. Because you totally are."

"Don't call me Jimmy, you evil whore. They have sake at this sushi place?" she asked, linking arms with Stacy. "Because I could use a couple."

"Or ten!"

"An even dozen," she agreed, and they laughed and left.

"The thing about sushi," Caitlyn sighed, walking Stacy to her car, "is that it's so completely delicious while you're eating it, but then when you're full—"

"You're like, *ewww,* I just ate a *ton* of raw fish!"

"And seaweed!"

"Exactly. I could barf right now. In fact . . ." Stacy looked anxiously over my shoulder. "Does my butt look fat in suede? Maybe I'll barf anyway."

"Don't you dare. Bulimia is so twentieth century." Caitlyn rolled her eyes. Stacy was one of those marvelous idiots who had no idea how fabulous they looked. She was five foot seven, just about the perfect

height for everything except professional basket-
ball, with out-of-control black hair and skin the color
of café au lait. She wore green contacts, truly striking in her high-cheekboned face. Caitlyn usually felt
like the village frump when she was out with her.
"Plus, we just dropped two hundred bucks on all
that fish. Don't waste it."

"I suppose. I'm doing an extra half hour on the
treadmill tomorrow though. What about you?"

*I can't. I've burned out the last three treadmills I tried.
Apparently, I can move faster than a Ford Mustang when
I set my mind to it.* "Um . . . I've been lifting weights
lately."

"Well, you look awesomely buff."

"Thanks."

"Seriously, Jimmy, what's up? You're not like yourself at all. I know the accident was a horror show, but
you seem totally fine now. I guess we both lucked
out." Stacy looked her over critically. "Better than
fine, actually. I don't think you've ever looked awe-
somer."

Caitlyn chose her words carefully. "Physically,
there isn't anything wrong with me."

"Then, what's up? I haven't seen you at a party
since the crash. The girls were talking about having, like, a reunion party, now that Shelly's off her
crutches and all—"

"It's a miracle we weren't all killed," she muttered. "Fucking miracle."

"Yup. Although it was tough work shaving my legs
when I got home—what is it *with* those hospital ra-
zors? You'd think a hospital would have, like, sharp
things. You shoulda seen my legs by the time I was
done. Total gross-out."

"What happened to you in the crash?"

Stacy smacked the top of her head. "Concussion, whiplash. The usual. Nothing you could see from the outside, and I had to wear this massively bogus neck brace for eight weeks, but I'm a lot better now. We all are, and like I said, we wanted to have, like, a reunion party, but we haven't been able to reach you and, like I said, there were all those totally lame rumors about you being dead."

"I've just been really busy with work." A lie. "I miss you guys though." The truth.

"Target acquired."

"What?"

"I didn't say anything."

"Alpha team, move in. Extreme caution."

"Are you okay, Caitlyn? You look kind of weird."

"Copy that."

"Can't you hear that?" Caitlyn asked, then realized instantly, of course Stacy couldn't hear it. *She* wasn't really hearing it either . . . it was like the mop-up team was talking in her head. That chip. That damn chip must be able to pick up their frequencies. And then broadcast it—uck!—into her brain.

Caitlyn felt a moment of panic. Sure, she was faster and stronger than regular people now, but she didn't have any training. Except in giving highlights and manicures. Unless the guys on the prowl needed haircuts, she was in deep shit.

She was simultaneously shocked and unsurprised. She'd been blowing off psychoboy for weeks and now it was time to dance. Those assfaces at O.S.F. had sent a whole team after her!

Talk about not taking no for an answer! She knew the unemployment rate was high for the state, but this was ridiculous.

She could hear them coming, moving quickly

and quietly—but not quietly enough, ha!—and wondered if it was better to just give up than risk getting some teeth knocked out. After suffering through junior high with braces, she wasn't about to risk the integrity of her mouth, thank you very—

Targets: 45° 72° 33°

Armed: .33 Beretta, full clip, none in the chamber

Armed: Mini UZI SMG, full clip, safety on

Armed: Semi-automatic Jericho pistol, full load, holstered. SAFETY IS OFF.

REPEAT, SAFETY IS OFF.

"What the hell?" she said out loud. This had happened to her so infrequently, she had succeeded in forgetting about it. Tough to do at the moment, since there were things in her left eye again. Not really in her eye . . . more like reading a page from a book . . . except the page was being projected inside her head. It was like those Terminator movies, when the audience could see through Arnold's eyes, kind of weird and cool at the same time, but how was she supposed to—

Targets: closing in. Engage. Engage. Engage.

"All right, all right. Don't *nag*." She kicked Stacy's feet out from under her, ignoring the woman's surprised squawk, and turned. She crossed the four-teen feet six inches between herself and Goon #1 in two point two seconds—

You can stop doing that now, computer chip. I'm on it.

Alas, stuck in her brain where it was, the thing wouldn't shut up.

It was good for one thing anyway. They weren't here to take her hard. Just take her.

She grinned—for the first time in days.

Too bad for them.

Later, Stacy was never quite sure what had happened on that side street. Her brainy, funky pal—God, Caitlyn had *always* been the *coolest*—had started talking to herself, then knocked her down. And before she could get up—heck, before she could roll over—Caitlyn was on the bad guys. She Sydney-Bristowed all over their asses and wasn't even out of breath when she finished!

And the funny thing—the extremely weird-but-cool thing—was that the bad guys were moving in slow motion compared to Caitlyn. It was like being an extra on *Buffy the Vampire Slayer*. Which kind of sucked, now that she thought about it, because she never pictured herself as the extra type, more like the supporting actress. Not the star, but important to the star, like Willow on *Buffy* or Elaine on *Seinfeld*.

Anyway, one of them flew almost all the way down the street and ended up flat on his back, right next to her. She got up in a hurry when she saw blood trickling out of his ear, and by then the other ones were down too.

And they looked *bad.* Like Colin Farrell in that too-cool S.W.A.T. movie. They were all scruffy and muscular and dressed in dark clothing and heavily armed—she counted three holsters on one of them. Empty holsters. Eh?

She turned and saw Jimmy walking toward her, her arms full of guns. "Sorry about that," she said, not sounding even a tiny bit sorry. "I wanted you down in case they got to their guns. I'll buy you a new skirt, okay?"

"Okay," she said automatically. "Um, this guy's bleeding. Out his *ear.*"

Caitlyn peered down at him, then blinked and—weird!—it almost looked like she was reading something. Except there wasn't anything to read. "It's okay," she said after a few moments. "He's got a concussion, but nothing's broken. He'll be out for a while, that's all. Serves them right anyway," she added defiantly. Almost—weird!—tearfully. Jimmy never cried. Not even that time when she got a B-on her trig final. Boy, *that* had been a tough day. "Besides, no means no, right? I mean, I don't *have* to work for anyone."

"Okay, Jimmy."

Caitlyn threw the guns down in a temper. They clattered to the street like ugly maracas. "I mean, jeez! I didn't *ask* them to fix me, did I?"

Stacy shook her head. "Nuh-uh."

"So they saved my life—big deal! What, now I'm a—an—an indentured servant for the rest of my life?"

"Doesn't seem like a great idea."

"Damn right! Shit! Shit on toast!"

"Yuck," Stacy said, which (whew!) made Caitlyn laugh. And thank God, because for a moment—a teensy moment, but still—she had been almost . . . what? Scared? Of *Caitlyn*? Not too stupid, because Jimmy was just about the nicest, coolest, sweetest—

Her friend stopped laughing and looked at her in a new way. And new, Stacy was starting to think, was bad. Very, very bad. "Look, Stace, you get home, okay?"

"Okay." Impulsively, she added, "You come with me, okay? Stay over for a while. We can stay up late and watch *Ocean's Eleven*—the George Clooney one, not the icky old one—and I'll call in sick tomorrow and we can hang out. It looks like you—like you could use a break. What do you say, Jimmy?"

"I say, don't call me Jimmy. It sounds like the best deal I've heard all damned month actually. But I can't."

"Why can't you?"

"I have to go see somebody first," she replied, sounding pissed all over again as she nudged the closest S.W.A.T. guy with the toe of her boot. "You go on. I'll get rid of the guns."

"Are you sure . . . ?"

"Just go."

"Well . . . okay. I—I'm glad you're better anyway."

"Oh, I'm better all right," she said morosely, bending to pick up the scary guns. "Better than ever. Too bad for me. But too bad for them, so that works out okay. You know?"

"Okay. I—g'night."

Stacy went home and took two Ambien, but it was hard to drop off just the same. She wished

Caitlyn had come home with her, but a tiny part of her—this was so lame it was hard to admit to herself, and she could never have said it out loud—was glad she hadn't.

Chapter 3

Caitlyn drove up on the lawn, plowed through the snow, parked on the freshly shoveled sidewalk, got out of her Intrepid, and marched over to the glass doors. She slammed her palm down on the touch plate and, big surprise, the doors unlocked.

There was nothing on the outside of the big glass building to indicate what it was—just the address, 2118, in four-foot-high numbers—on the inside. The security guards stood behind their granite desk when she entered, but neither came near her. Good for them.

"Evening, Miss James," one of them said.

"Is he in?" she asked.

"Uh, yeah. Top floor. He's—"

"*Don't* say he's expecting me."

"Well," the other guard said apologetically, "he kind of is. Did you really take out an entire extractment team by yourself? Because that's—"

She had already stomped across the black marble floor and was in the stairwell, and didn't hear the rest. Damned if she was going to be trapped in one of their stupid elevators. She'd seen enough TV movies to know that was a bad idea, thanks very much!

Instead, she took the fifteen flights in about sixty seconds and popped out in the hallway, not even out of breath.

Okay, so. There were *some* benefits. And it beat being dead. Mostly.

But still. No meant no.

She was in an area she thought of as done up in Expensive Boring Office. Dark wood, dark carpet, light blue water cooler. The desks were also dark wood and looked like they'd been mass-produced and then delivered on the same day. The place smelled like paper and coffee grounds.

"Ah, Miss James! The Boss has been expecting you." It was always like that, *just* like that. . . . The Boss. You could hear the capital letter. "Some coffee? Tea?"

"No."

"He's finishing up right now with the senator from Wisconsin—"

"At nine o'clock at night?"

"The Boss works long hours," the secretary said with weird pride, "but if you'll—"

Caitlyn kicked the door in. It was easy. It shot off its hinges and slammed into the thick carpet. It sounded like a woman beating a rug—*whumpf!* And it was *so* easy. That was, in a lot of ways, the scariest part of all that had happened to her. Been done to her. How easy it was to use it. The technology. It was exactly like using her own muscles, her own brain.

She had never been able to see where she stopped and the nanobytes began.

"Caitlyn James to see you, sir," his secretary said, peeking around her and not missing a beat.

The senator—a tall, good-looking woman with dark hair coiled on top of her head, shot up from her seat, and papers went flying.

"We'll pick this up tomorrow, Nancy," the Boss said. "I'm afraid I've got a scheduling conflict right now."

"No doubt," she said, leaving the file and picking her way past the door.

"Love your hair," Caitlyn said as the senator passed her.

"What can I do for you, Caitlyn?" the Boss said, sitting back down and folding his hands on his immaculate desk blotter. He was short, in his forties, but powerfully built through the shoulders. He was dressed in a black suit—a good one, probably Italian—and his hair was the same shade, slicked back from his forehead. His eyes were the color of dirty ice, and his eyebrows were so light as to be invisible. As a result, he looked like a mean egg.

"You can die slowly, coughing your guts out in a part of the world that hasn't heard of morphine."

The Boss blinked slowly, like a lizard. "I'll get right on that. I take it our team earned your enmity?"

"*You've* earned my en—my em—you're the one I'm pissed at!"

"Caitlyn, Caitlyn," he sighed, shaking his head as if over a daughter missing curfew. She hated that. The fatherly thing. *So* lame. If he'd been her father, she would have had a Clorox cocktail before she hit puberty. "We've been over this before. You work for the O.S.F. now."

"No, I do *not*. I already told you. I'm not going to work for you guys. I don't even know what O.S.F. means."

"Office of Scientific Findings. And yes. You do. We *own* you." He smiled, revealing very white teeth. "Want to see the receipt?"

"Drop dead, you bloodless bastard."

"Such a lack of gratitude, considering that we saved your life. Three times, if the reports are correct. And they always are."

She was silent, thinking, *I never asked you to. Never, not one time.* The question was, would she rather be dead than under the Boss's thumb?

And here was what kept her up nights: Could they undo what they had done? Push a button from H.Q. and zap all the nanobytes into oblivion?

Could she go on if they did that? Go back to being normal? As normal as she had ever been anyway?

Annoyingly, he was still talking. "Caitlyn, dear, we've spent a *fortune* on you. A bloody fortune. If we traded you, we could get Alaska in exchange."

"So? I didn't ask you to save me. You were snooping all the channels, looking for a guinea pig. Some no-nothing loser—"

"Don't be so hard on yourself, darling."

"—to tinker and fiddle with and—and *change*."

"For the better, which you seem not to have noticed."

"Don't expect my goddamned gratitude, you snake. Just because you've souped me up a bit, I'm supposed to do your dirty work? Fuck you."

"Yes, so you've said. However, free will—at least

in the O.S.F.—is an illusion. We work for a higher power here, Caitlyn. Your—how did you put it? Your indentured servitude is necessary so millions of Americans can enjoy their freedom. When you think about it," he added, sighing again, "you seem awfully selfish."

"Pal, you haven't seen the least of it."

"Think of the havoc you could wreak on terrorism if you only applied yourself."

"Think of the havoc I could wreak on your lungs if I only applied myself."

"This attitude of yours . . . I've given you time to see things in a more mature and, shall we say, less stupid manner—"

"Blow me."

"It's too bad." He pressed a button on his desk. She could hear a hissing sound, like a snake caught in the ventilation shaft.

Warning. Warning. Unidentified gas in the vicinity.

Analyzing: three parts gas to one hundred parts room air. Dispensing nanobytes to lungs to facilitate oxygen extraction.

"I hope, after you've rested, we can begin anew. With a fresh attitude. This tiresome squabbling is getting us nowhere. Really, it's—why are you still conscious?"

"Oh, I've been holding my breath," she said. It had been surprisingly easy. "I can do it until I need to leave, which is right now."

"Hmmmm." He pushed another button, and the hissing stopped. "Just as well. Some of that was going to float over here, and I didn't want to go to the trouble of finding my mask in this mess." He indicated the piles of files. "Caitlyn, I'll be honest with you—"

"After you just squirted knockout gas at me? And who *does* that, by the way? It's like I'm trapped in a bad episode of *The Bionic Woman*!"

"Oh, it is not! Stop being so dramatic. Just last week I knocked out the Speaker of the House. Now, be fair. When have I ever misled you?"

"Go on," she grumbled.

"Very good. You are the first of your kind, a fully functioning cybernetic organism who has retained your humanity. More, you are a *human* cybernetic organism, and thus you are held back only by the limitations of your own mind."

He seemed to expect her to say something, but she had no comment. Frankly, she wasn't quite sure where he was going with any of this.

"Simply put," he continued, "we don't know your limits. I suspect you don't either. You shouldn't have been able to analyze the gas so quickly, but you did. You shouldn't have been able to disarm our team so quickly, but you did. And this with no formal training! Needless to say, the fact that you are more than you were is a tremendous validation of our work. The nanobytes we—"

"Infected me with."

"—placed within you are now as much a part of you as your heart, your lungs, your delightfully annoying personality. We need you, Caitlyn. We must have you, in fact."

"I think I liked it better when you were spraying gas." That was nothing but the truth. His honesty was horrifying. It was awful to find out someone you couldn't stand would do anything to hang on to you.

"You were very expensive, but that's not the least of it. There are men in this world who make me look like the late, lamented Mister Rogers. Men who would gut and rape your friend Stacy and then sit down to a steak dinner. Men who would do that on a global scale if given the chance. We have to stop them. We need you to do it."

"But I—I never wanted to be a spy. I don't know anything about it and I don't think I'd be good at it. Seriously, Eggman, you don't want *me*."

"Well, we have you. And you know more than you think. You won't give off 'spy vibes,' for want of a better phrase, so you can go places many of our operatives can't. Who will suspect a comely, giddy twenty-five-year-old of being a government assassin?"

"Twenty-four," she said automatically. Then, "Whoa, *whoa*. I'm not killing anybody, pal. *No way*."

"I'll let you decide that," he said generously, "when the time comes."

"You're scaring the shit out of me."

"I've been known to have that effect on young women."

She shuddered. *Ick!* "What if we make a deal, O short, dark, and evil one?"

"I'm listening, O annoying, tall, and orange-haired one."

"*One* job. Just one. Pick your biggest badass, and I'll go after him. Take him out, stop him from blowing up the world, bitch-slap him, whatever. And then we're quits. You saved my life, I saved your job. We're even. We're done."

"That sounds fine."

"What? Really? It does?"

"Yes."

"Huh. According to the chip in my head, you're telling the truth."

"I'm sure this isn't the first time you've heard voices in your head." He rose and extended his hand. She shook it, ignoring the urge to squeeze until bone splinters appeared and he screamed and screamed. *Maybe next time.* "Welcome aboard, Caitlyn. We'll be in touch."

God help me.

Part Two

Chapter 4

Caitlyn walked into Magnifique, noting with approval that every seat had a butt in it. She had used her inheritance to buy it as soon as she got out of college, and it was one of the most popular hair salons in St. Paul. It was her sweetheart, her baby. She'd been away too long.

And she figured the quickest way to get back to normal was to, well, *be* normal. Which meant getting back to Mag's day-to-day running, pronto.

"Jenny," she said, and the receptionist waved, turned her head to the left, and tapped her headset, which was so small, Caitlyn never knew if she was on the phone or not.

". . . uh-huh . . . yes, we've got you down for next Saturday at two o'clock . . . uh-huh . . . yep, highlights, lowlights, and a cut . . . well, we'll see you then." She punched a button on her console and smiled up at Caitlyn. "Hey, chief. What's up?"

"We're overbooked again, that's what's up. Bad, *bad* Jenny."

"Oh, come on. You're the one always complaining when there isn't 'a butt in every seat.' "

Caitlyn was momentarily startled when the chip in her head reported Jenny's blood pressure and pulse, but she rallied quickly when it pointed out that Jenny was mildly stressed. "We are not Northwest, Jenny. Stop double-booking."

"Yes, ma'am."

She knew the younger woman was appropriately cowed, so she didn't push. "And the highlights look great."

Jenny smiled. "I'm a walking ad for this place, and you know it."

"I do know it." Jenny really was. Small, skinny, with shoulder-length blond hair (and red highlights now) and greenish blue eyes, Jenny was ridiculously pretty, one of those women who always looked effortlessly "done." Which, of course, was not why Caitlyn had given her the job, but it certainly didn't hurt. "Where's the mail?"

Jenny reached beneath her desk and withdrew a box, which was overflowing. Caitlyn eyed it with distaste. "Paperless office, my big white butt."

"Chief, if we could just go one workday without talking about your butt . . ."

"Yeah, yeah."

"And here comes your ten o'clock."

Caitlyn turned in time to nearly get knocked off her feet by the exuberance of her client's greeting. "Caitlyn! Thank God you're here! I was worried you were still out!"

"Hi, Karen."

"Not that I have a problem with any of your girls, but you really get me! And I've got a signing tonight! And as you can see, the situation is dire!"

"It's not that bad," she replied, inspecting the other woman's roots. Karen was, unfortunately, both a close talker and incapable of communicating in a normal speaking voice. The combination meant Caitlyn usually bent back a good six inches when Karen was chatting, and eventually clawed for the Advil. "We'll neaten up these ends for you, and that'll make a big difference."

"Great! Let's do it!"

"Okay." Caitlyn waited while Karen hung up her coat, then walked her over to the chair. Caitlyn's throne/home-away-from-home was in the perfect location—she could do heads while keeping an eye on the others, observe Jenny's phone manner, and know when the mail showed up. Also, the drawers were wide and deep, and stored many things.

"Let's get started. What do you think about covering the gray and maybe lightening up this brown with some goldish highlights?"

"I think that sounds great! But anything will be a vast improvement!"

"Oh, cut that out. You're too hard on yourself." Karen was an attractive, plump thirty-five, but she disliked looking her age. "Tonight's the signing?"

"Yes! I'm a nervous wreck!"

Yikes. Karen's volume rose in direct proportion to her emotional state. She did PR, and most of her clients were local writers. "It'll go great. You've planned the heck out of it."

"That's true!"

"I'm just gonna get a couple of Advil." Caitlyn rummaged in the top drawer, then paused. She hadn't been sick a single day since the government cheerfully infected her with nanobytes. Not a cold, not a headache.

Karen would be the definitive test. If she didn't have a skull buster after doing Karen's head, she would never have one.

Find out once and for all, Caitlyn thought. *Am I a true freak, or is there a chance that things could ever get back to normal?*

"So where have you been?! We've all wondered!"

"Visiting friends around the country. On second thought, I'll pass on the Advil. So," Caitlyn prompted, picking up a comb, "tell me about tonight. In vast, lengthy detail."

Chapter 5

"**I**'m a freak," she told Stacy over strawberry daiquiris that night.

"So?" Stacy replied, waving the waitress over. "Two more of these, please," she said, pointing to their half-empty glasses. "Hey, how's the baby?"

"Fat," the waitress replied. *Carrie* was stitched over her left breast in red thread. "Colic's done, thank God. Now I don't have to worry about dropping him off at the county."

"Even better, now you can have him over," Stacy replied promptly, which made the waitress crack up.

Caitlyn shook her head. Stacy knew every waitress, bellboy, waiter, cook, chef, Mall of America employee, and dry cleaner in Minneapolis. She never forgot a face, a name, an offspring, or a discount. And she *hadn't* been infected with nanobytes. Truly inspirational.

"So, you're a freak," Stacy said when the waitress had left. "What else is new?"

"Not the only girl in the sorority who knew who Nietzsche was, was a freak. *Freak* freak."

"Again: so?"

Caitlyn sighed noisily, trying to suppress her annoyance. "So, what am I supposed to do about it?"

"Does this have something to do with the fact that you own Mag instead of just being the manager like everyone thinks?"

"No. I went back today, by the way. Place is doing great."

"Of course it's doing great. You give free manicures while your customers are waiting for their hair to cook, so why wouldn't it do great?"

She grinned in spite of herself. "We in the trade prefer 'foil technique' to 'cook.' And tell me that wasn't a great idea."

"Yeah, yeah, it was a great idea. Back to your freakish nature, which is nothing new, FYI. Does this have something to do with your Houdini last fall?"

"Yes."

"Okay. So, what happened?"

"You'd never believe it."

"Hey, I believed you wanted to switch from psych to econ."

"This is somewhat different," Caitlyn said.

"And I believed you when you said you wanted to buy Mag and do heads and run your own business, when your folks had left you so much money, you'd never have to work again."

"Again, that doesn't really fall into the realm of the unbelievable."

"And I believed you when you put most of your inheritance into a trust for that charity The Foot, which means they get to spend the interest, and you can't ever touch the principle. Of your own money!

Which means that the richest twenty-something in Minneapolis often eats ramen for supper."

"Hey, you can get five packs of them for eighty-five cents," Caitlyn said.

"So I *know* you're a freak, okay? I've known for years. What, you're trying to shock me now?" Stacy took a slurp of her old drink, then turned her attention to the new one. "Mmmm, strawberries. Go on, then. Shock me."

"Well, I'm supposed to work for the government now. They did me a favor and now I'm supposed to do them a favor."

"Oh. Well, I figured it was something like that. Is that why you're looking so buff? You're like Sydney Bristow on *Alias* . . . normal on the outside, and buff on the outside, but you know all this extra stuff too."

"Nothing at all like *Alias*." She was pretty sure. As usual, a conversation with Stacy involving alcohol was confusing and soothing. "But yeah, it's why I'm looking so buff. Let's put it this way: I was sick—"

"More like seriously fucked-up from the accident."

"Right. And they helped me get better, and now they're saying they didn't help me for free."

"Well, *nothing's* free."

"Come on, Stace . . ."

She chewed on her garnish and stared at Caitlyn with a gaze so direct, it was almost frightening. "Nothing's free, Jimmy. Not one thing. You're rich, but you have no family. I've got a family, and can't stand to be around them. And Joanie . . . you remember Joanie?"

"Art major."

"Yup. She could draw anything, anything in the world. And she'd have four skull-busting migraines a week. That was the trade-off. Draw like Da Vinci, cry like my little sister when the pain comes. Nothing's free."

"Stacy, for a supposed ditz, you've got a disturbingly practical streak."

"Uh-huh. So, do them the favor. Get square, and get out."

She sighed. "That's the plan. I think. I mean, I agreed to do this one thing for them. Except . . . I don't think getting out will be so easy."

"Is this about that test you took so you could be a mailman? Mailwoman? That civil service what-d'you-call-it?"

"No. Although, FYI, I got the highest score in the state."

"Yeah, yeah, you're brilliant, big deal."

"And I have no idea if it would be hard to get free of the U.S. Post Office." Although, for future reference, that whole "government service thing" would be an excellent excuse. Not that she was looking for one. But just in case. "I'm just not sure I want to get wrapped up with these jerks."

"Cautious is prob'ly the way to go," Stacy agreed.

"Let's put it this way: they helped me to help themselves. It really didn't have anything to do with *me*. So why should I do anything for them?"

" 'Cuz they *did* help you. I'm not sure it matters why if it was something to your benefit."

"Hmm," Caitlyn said, and changed the subject.

Chapter 6

"Neutralize," she said to the man who would never be her boss.

"Yeah," the Boss said. "Neutralize. I want this little punk stomped on."

She was in the place she'd swore she'd never return to, then swore she'd return to only once. She didn't touch the coffee the Boss's assistant had brought her. She didn't make a move toward the chair the Boss had offered her. "Stomped on."

"Yes, Caitlyn, I'd be tempted to ask if you're hard of hearing, except I know you're far from it. *Stomped on.* In the last nine weeks he's come up with the Hello Kitty virus, the Kiss Me virus, and the Do Me virus."

"Heh," she said, though it wasn't very funny. She'd managed to avoid two of them, but Do Me had infected her hard drive with porn.

"We've tracked him down, and for your first assignment—"

"First? Boy, were *you* not paying attention last time."

"—I want you to neutralize him."

What, he thinks I can't crack his code? Neutralize. Ha. "This is what the O.S.F. spends its time and money on?"

"If my computer sends one more picture of a hum job to my sister-in-law," the Boss said through gritted teeth, "I will *not* be responsible for what happens next."

"This time," Caitlyn said, doing her Steven Seagal squint, "it's personal."

"And another thing. I've been paging you for eighteen hours. Where the hell have you been?"

"A party."

He frowned at her. She thought. His smooth forehead didn't wrinkle at all. Botox? Deal with the devil?

"Okay, well, now that you work for me, you're supposed to lie and say something like your pager was broken, so I don't think you were blowing me off."

"It's working fine."

He narrowed his dirty-water-colored eyes at her. He was dressed in another dark suit today. She didn't know if he had one, or twenty. "Caitlyn, you'd better cut the shit."

"Not part of our deal," she said, and got up and walked out. She was meanly glad to see he hadn't replaced his door.

The evil genius who had violated over a million computers lived in a red brick split-level in Chicago, Illinois. The O.S.F. plane had her there in about seventy minutes.

There was a car waiting to whisk her from the

tarmac to the house, and while she made small talk with the driver, she couldn't help but wonder if all these people knew what she was, and what she was going to do.

"No," the driver, a heavyset woman in her fifties with red curly hair and laugh lines, replied in response to her question. "We're just supposed to take you from point A to point B and back to point A whenever you're finished. You know, finished with whatever it is you need to finish. Then back you go for a debriefing."

"Debriefing? Like, I tell the Boss everything that happened?"

"Exactly."

"Because I'm not going back there. Ever."

The driver had no response to that, then said, "You're definitely the youngest agent I've ever squired around."

"Thanks."

"Too young by far, if you ask me, I don't know what the Boss is thinking."

"I'm not *that* young," she pointed out. "I finished college. I'm Caitlyn, by the way."

"Mmmf," the driver said.

"See, what happens is, then you give me your name."

"It's Sharon."

"Well, nice to meet you, Sharon. Thanks for the ride, I guess."

Sharon rolled her eyes, then pulled up to the split-level. Eight one three Feather Avenue. "Here we go."

"You drive right up to the front door?"

"What, I'm supposed to drop you off a block away? It's pouring out."

"Just doesn't seem very, uh, spylike."

"Well, it is. Now go in there and shoot him in the face."

"*What?*"

The driver flapped a hand in her direction. "Or, you know, whatever it is you need to do."

"Jeez," she muttered, and opened the door. "I'll be back in—I have no idea."

"I'll be here."

Caitlyn slammed the car door shut and headed up the sidewalk. This was extremely weird, and not at all like spy games on television. Did she knock on the door or kick it down or ring the bell or sneak around back or what? This was *so* weird.

She was stretching out her hand to ring the bell when the door opened, and she was nearly knocked off the steps by an older woman in an obvious hurry.

"Sorry, dear, didn't see you."

"I'm looking for T—"

"Yes, yes, he's in the basement, go on in, dear. I've got to run to the store and then get my tires rotated. . . . I'll be back in a couple of hours."

And she charged down the sidewalk, jumped into her Ford Escape, and squealed out of the driveway.

I'm supposed to kill this guy while his mommy's shopping?

She thought it over for a minute, then went into the house.

Chapter 7

"Hellooooooo?" She went down the stairs. There was only one life sign in the basement, and he was focused on the computer. He wasn't remotely nervous, or even anxious. In fact, he didn't seem to care that she was there at all.

She waited for the chip in her head to give her some advice, or at least a readout, but nothing. *Nada.* Maybe it was taking a break.

"Ma, I said I needed more Hot Pockets and that was it," he said without turning around. "C'mon, I gotta work."

"Yes, well, um, I'm here to put an end to your, um, evil ways. And stuff."

He turned around and gaped at her. Terrance Filit was the stereotypical nerd—thick glasses, *Star Trek* T-shirt, faded jeans, skinny bod—but he had the biggest, bluest eyes she'd ever seen. Paul Newman eyes. Or creepy-kid-from-Godsend eyes, if you wanted to get really picky . . .

"Are you looking for my mom?" he asked, dazzled.

She smiled. Luckily, she'd taken the time to do some red lowlights in contrast with her white blond strands. The Boss could say what he wanted, but he could never say she'd gone on assignment not looking her best. "No, I passed her on the way out. I was sent here from an elite government agency to . . . never mind, it sounds lame even before I say it out loud."

"God, you're really tall."

"Thanks." She crossed her arms over her chest and looked stern. "Look, you gotta quit with the viruses, okay? I mean, a couple of them were funny, but people can't work. Think if you came home and your computer was totally on the fritz. It would, like, totally disrupt your life."

"I'd love to come home and find my computer was stuffed with porn," he confessed. "It's better than—" Terry reddened and looked away. "Never mind."

Neutralize him, the Boss said in her head. Creepy. That better not be her chip. If he had access to her chip, she was kicking his ass severe.

He'd love to come home and find his computer stuffed with porn?

The viruses were all pornographic in nature . . . if your hard drive got infected, it pulled all sorts of porn from the Web and dumped it into your drive. Or, worse, had everyone in your e-mail box e-mail you porn. It was kind of funny, just the sort of thing a kid—a *boy*—would find amusing.

A boy so focused on porn because he had no experience with the real thing, and as a result was massively curious as well as massively—

She unbuttoned her coat. "Mind if I stay a few minutes?"

"Are you going to shoot me?" he gasped.

"No."

Thirty-six seconds later

"Wow!" Terry cried. "That was just so totally *wow!*"

"You're uh, eighteen, right?" *I didn't just commit statutory rape, right?*

"Nineteen in June. Um. That was so . . . I gotta get in the Darth chat room and tell all the guys!"

"Yes, yes. Now, listen. You can't design any more of these—"

"Who wants to do that now?" he said impatiently, waving at his computer and looking generally disgusted. "I've got other stuff to worry about. You've—you've opened up a whole new world for me! I'll never design another virus again!"

That sure sounded like neutralized to her. Good 'nuf. "Alrighty, then," she said, slipping into her panties, leggings, bra, and cashmere turtleneck. She pulled on her wool socks and stepped into her boots. "Make sure you keep your word, or I'll have to come back and, um, neutralize you again."

He nearly fell off the couch they'd dallied on. "Really?"

"Shut up, Terry," she said kindly, and shrugged into her coat and walked out.

Chapter 8

"You—you—you—you—you—"
Caitlyn studied her nails and decided she could go one more day without a touch-up. "Me—me—me—me—me what? Can you hurry this up, please? I've got to be at Mag in another half hour."

"He's not dead," the Boss growled.

"Well, he was sleepy when I left . . ."

He cursed her, but since she was raised by an alcoholic Air Force sergeant, she was used to it, and could barely conceal a yawn. "And now I'm done, right? Right. And by the way, it was a major creep-out to have your driver bring me *here*. Like you don't have my home address? So, I'll—"

"We'll be in touch," he interrupted. "But you should leave—before I shoot you in the head."

"Why?" she asked suspiciously.

He balled up an interdepartmental memo and took a bite out of it, then spat the paper wad into his wastebasket. *What a revolting habit,* she thought, amazed.

"Because I'm really annoyed that you didn't kill that kid," he snapped.

"No, why will you be in touch?"

"Oh, you know. This and that." He grinned, showing flecks of paper on his teeth. "Maybe you'll need a tune-up."

"*One* job, remember?"

"I never forget anything."

"Well, thanks to you guys," she said bitterly, "now neither do I."

"You just never know what may come up," he went on cheerfully. A cheerfully psychotic asshole in charge of a top-secret government facility. Oh, this was gonna be one for the journal. "Nobody can predict the future, you know. Not even you, sunshine."

"Do *not* call me sunshine. And could you go back to yelling? I find it less creepy than your fake 'we all get along great' thing."

"And you're getting only half your salary for this one," he added, "since Terrance Filit is still alive."

"Oh, I'm getting paid? Right." She mulled that one over for a minute. Drawing a check for this crap was something she hadn't considered. Of course, government salary. How great could it be? But still. The bennies were probably pretty good. "This is my cue to say Keep your dirty money, except my rent is late."

"Half," he said again, looking meaner than ever. "And the next time I send you to neutralize somebody, make sure they go to sleep dead, okay?"

"I have no idea what that means, but fortunately, there won't be a next time. Right? Right. Besides, if you don't quit bugging me, I'm going to tell."

"Tell?" He eyed the crumpled-up memo, then threw the whole thing in the garbage without eating any more of it, to her relief. "As in tattle? You're going to tattle on the O.S.F.?"

He was so sneery about it, she hesitated before saying, "That's right. I'll tell everyone what you guys did to me. Without my permission, I might add. I mean, come on. Monitoring police bands and hospital radios? And scooping up the first almost-dead person you find and infecting her with God-knows-what? Who *does* that?"

"We do," he said. "Check our charter."

"I'll—I'll call a press conference and—and you'll be toast." As if she had the slightest idea how to call a press conference. Maybe she'd just take a jaunt down to the *Star Tribune* offices and do a demonstration for them. Then *they* would call the press conference. Right? Right.

The Boss was laughing at her. His eyebrows had smoothed out, but his face was still an alarming shade of brick. "Tell!" he gasped, waving at her. "Tell!"

"Excuse me?"

"Tell whomever you want. Tell Stacy. Tell your mailman. Tell your landlord. Tell the president, that fucking moron. *We* don't care."

"Well, why don't you?" she asked, nettled.

"Caitlyn, dear child—"

"Do *not* call me that."

"—what would they do? Even if they believed you? Do you think Stacy would tell the world even if she had the faintest idea how? Do you think your mailman gives a ripe shit? I've got a little test for you—tonight, when you're out having drinks or premarital sex or whatever it is you do to pass the time, yell to the bar that you're the product of a secret government experiment. See what happens."

"But . . ." She was totally floored. She had figured the Boss was evil—he wore too much brown—but she never would have guessed he was suicidally careless. "But in the movies, blowing your cover, that's always a huge disaster. It—"

"Sunshine, do you see a movie set anywhere?"

"Do *not*—"

"This is real life, and let me tell you something about your fellow homo dumbasses: they're too wrapped up in their own problems to give a fuck about anything that may or may not have happened to you."

"I'm sure that's not right," she said stiffly.

The Boss shrugged.

She stood abruptly, resisted the urge to grab him by the ears and pound his head into the desk for ten, maybe twenty minutes, and walked to the doorway.

"Don't screw up next time!" he called after her.

"Blow me next time," she muttered.

She thought she heard laughter when she headed into the stairwell, but though she strained, she couldn't make it out. She decided it was her imagination.

Chapter 9

As she stepped into Mag, she overheard some of her regulars playing her all-time favorite, Mother-in-law Jeopardy. She grinned as she hung her coat in the back, then hurried over to her chair, where Jenny had already sent her first customer of the afternoon.

"I'll take 'you did not just say that to me' for two hundred, Alex," her client, Lydia, was saying, dropping her purse on the floor and waving to Caitlyn.

"The answer is 'Where your son will spend eternity.' "

"The question is 'What is hell,' " Lydia replied promptly, "because he doesn't go to Sunday school."

"Ding-ding-ding-ding!" Caro, Robbie, and Barb all clapped. Robbie, the game-show host, added, "Very good, Lydia, and that puts you in the lead."

Caitlyn smirked and started combing out Mag's running Mother-in-law Jeopardy champ. Squeaky clean, as usual. Lydia had a thing about never coming to the salon with hair that needed to be washed.

Her mom had done heads back in the day and would have skinned her alive if she'd shown up at a salon with greasy hair.

" 'Lo, Caitlyn. Alex, I'll take 'things that caused my mother-in-law to freak out for no reason,' for four hundred."

"The question is 'What your son had for breakfast one day.' "

"Um . . . what is cereal without milk?"

"Ennnnnnhhhhh! I'm sorry, Lydia. Barb?"

"What is toast?"

"Ding-ding-ding! Good job, Barb. And the board goes to—ouch, Dara, not so hard."

"Sorry," Dara replied, easing up with the comb.

"I'll take 'you told your mother I'd do *what?*' for six hundred, Alex."

"Something you swore you'd never do."

"What is host Easter?"

"That is correct, Barb!"

"You guys," Caitlyn said, shaking her head. "C'mon, married life can't be that bad."

"Talk to us when you're married," Barb said. "Love the highlights, by the way."

"Thanks."

"Why don't you keep them for a while?"

Caitlyn blinked, confused. "Because I don't know what tomorrow will bring?" she guessed as if it were a riddle.

"You have ADD hair," Robbie pointed out. She was younger than Caitlyn, a PhD candidate at the U of M. A nerd who cared about her appearance . . . a rare and wonderful thing. "I'm here every six weeks, and you never have the same hair color twice in a row."

"I try to match my hair," she explained, "to what the situation demands."

"Medical boards," Robbie said.

"Dark brown with reddish gold highlights, wire-rim glasses."

"But you don't wear glasses."

"The lenses," she explained, snipping Lydia's bangs, "are clear."

"Dinner at the White House."

"Dark blond hair, red lipstick."

"Uh . . . job interview."

"Brown hair, bangs, minimal makeup."

"Class reunion."

"Which one?"

"Uh . . . tenth."

"Bright red hair, lots of makeup."

"But, Caitlyn," Lydia said, "isn't your natural hair color that gorgeous white blond? Marilyn Monroe blond?"

"Yes."

"Why, *why* would you ever color it? Women pay a hundred bucks to color their hair to match what God gave you."

She shrugged. She was looking for something, had been all her life. Too bad she didn't have a clue what it was. And too bad she kept expecting to find it in the mirror. "I like change, I guess."

Robbie was still trying to stump her. "Dinner with an ex-boyfriend."

"Black streaks, perfect makeup. Engagement ring."

"Your wedding."

"Natural. No color, but flawless makeup and ex-pensive underwear. Maybe a Vera Wang dress."

"Get-together with old sorority girlfriends." A new voice, one she didn't recognize. She looked across the room and saw a new customer sitting patiently with her hair in foils. She was small, about five feet tall, with brown eyes and long lashes. She was pretending to read that week's *People*, but Caitlyn could tell she wasn't cognitively engaged in the magazine. She was much more interested in the conversation. "With lots of alcohol and a rented limo."

"Dark blond streaks," she replied. "Miniskirt, fitted T-shirt, sandals."

The woman just smiled in response.

"I've never seen you in here before," Caitlyn said pleasantly.

"I heard this place was the best. So here I am."

"Mmmm. Well, we appreciate that. Don't we, girls?"

The other cutters murmured in response, and Dara struck up a conversation with the stranger. Who was so obviously a spy, it wasn't even funny.

Great. The Boss's way of keeping an eye on her, she supposed.

"Oh, and I've got one for Mother-in-law Jeopardy," the stranger added.

"Sorry," Caitlyn said shortly. "Game's over."

Chapter 10

"—So then the Boss is all shoot-him-in-the-face and I'm all screw-that-buddy-roo, and he's all just-do-it, you know, like a Nike ad gone mad, and I'm all *you*-just-do-it-you're-so-fond-of-guns, and he's all— *unf!*"

The second punching bag's chain snapped and it sailed a good six feet in the air before collapsing on the mat.

"Aw, nuts!"

"Now you're just showing off," Stacy said. She was dressed in trendy workout gear—tight shorts, two tank tops (one pink, one white), spotless white socks, spotless workout shoes—and sipped her daiquiri (she'd brought a cooler full of them) while she watched Caitlyn work out. "Seriously, knock it off. It's bad enough I'm already the 'funny one.' I gotta be the 'dull one' too?"

"Shut up, you're gorgeous, dammit, dammit!" Caitlyn kicked the now-supine punching bag, which obligingly rolled over and over. "So I, the new kid, cleverly think up a way to fix the virus problem without *anybody* getting shot in the face—"

"You've been using that phrase a lot," Stacy observed, pushing the pedals of her stationary bike hard enough so they went around once, then slowly stopped. She rewarded her exertions with another gulp of alcohol and ice. "It's kind of yucky."

"—and for my thanks I get a bunch of veiled threats and he *laughs* at me."

"Sounds like a real jerk."

"A real jerk*off.* Yes. He is, he *is*! And I can't work out anymore! I wreck half the gym!"

"Oh, please." Stacy rolled her eyes. "Pardon me if I don't cry you a river. It just means you can't kickbox anymore."

"But it's, like, *the* best way to stay in shape."

"I don't think staying in shape is gonna be your big concern anymore," Stacy observed. "Flabby thighs are now the least of your problems. And it's one o'clock in the morning, in case you didn't notice. We're the only ones in the gym except for the—"

"What happened here?" the trainer cried, rushing up to them.

Caitlyn opened her mouth to say that she did not know, when Stacy interrupted. "This *thing* fell down and almost *hit* my *friend.*"

"Oh my God. Oh my God! I'm so sorry! Are you all right?"

"She's fine," Stacy answered, again before Caitlyn could say a word. "She's got the reflexes of a cat on crack."

"Look," Caitlyn continued when the trainer had hurried to the back to fill out the appropriate forms, "you seem a little, I don't know, cavalier about what's happened to me. What they *did* to me. Where's the outrage on my behalf? Where's the love, Stace?"

Stacy climbed off the bike, smoothed her hair back, checked her reflection in one of the mirrors, then replied, "Am I sorry you got hurt? Sure am. Am I sorry you're in this weird-ass fix? Yup. Am I sorry you're still alive, and better than ever, and nobody can push you around anymore, not that they really ever did, excluding your parents, God rest 'em? No."

"I'm having a little trouble following that," she admitted.

"It's like this, Jimmy. The first time I called the hospital—you know, after they'd released me and I was home? I wanted to check up on you, right? Well, they told me you were dead. And I—it freaked me out, okay? It totally, completely freaked me out. I wasn't ready to lose my best friend in my mid-twenties, okay? I mean, I heard later that it was a mistake and you were in rehab or whatever, but still. That first time. Hearing it. Major *major* shock."

"Sorry," Caitlyn said quietly. She'd been so focused on what had happened to her, she had never considered what had happened to her friend.

"Wasn't *your* fault. Anyway, now I don't have to worry about that happening—you doing the big gak—for a long time. So I guess if you're looking for a shoulder to cry on, you'd better talk to somebody who doesn't care either way if you're dead. Which ain't me."

"That's . . . so sweet," she said at last. "I'm pretty sure. So the sympathy train is at an end, huh?"

"Baby, the train never left the station." Stacy sat on the floor, leaned against one of the rolled-up mats, propped one toe atop the other toe, took another sip, wriggled her shoulders, then asked, "So, what else can you do?"

"Burn out that bike. Knock the last kicking bag off the chain. Pick up every weight in this place—at the same time."

"So, standard stuff. Ah, but can you do this?" She set her drink down, then patted her stomach and rubbed her head at the same time.

Caitlyn burst out laughing. "No, they must have left that out of the upgrade."

"Well, then," Stacy said, clearly trying not to sound smug, and failing miserably.

Chapter 11

Caitlyn hung up her coat and glared at the spy, who claimed her name was Sara. Sara hauled her sorry butt into Mag about once a week, which in itself was a joke. Caitlyn was a big believer in maintenance, feeling every woman should try to look her best, but even her most hard-core clients contented themselves with semi-monthly visits. Some secret-secret-ultra-cool government spy agency if they didn't know that most basic spa-ism.

Thus far, "Sara" had been in for a pedicure, to have a broken nail fixed—Caitlyn didn't know if she'd cracked it herself or if it had been an accident . . . probably the former—a haircut, highlights, a deep conditioning treatment, and another haircut. Then another manicure and pedicure. It was springtime now, and Caitlyn couldn't help wondering how the powers that be decided Sara would pretend to be a customer *that* week. Acne attack? More broken nails? Foot fungus? Bikini wax? It would have been funny if it weren't so damn annoying.

She hadn't heard from O.S.F. or the Boss since she'd un-virgined (de-virgined?) Terry, a blessing for which she gave thanks daily. She supposed she should be waiting for the other shoe to drop, but she was too busy pretending everything was back to normal. It was much easier to pull that off when she didn't have to deal with, speak to, or look at the Boss.

Sara the spy was chatting with Dara—Sara and Dara . . . how too fucking cute—about a new look. Since she'd had four new looks in as many weeks, Dara had told Caitlyn in privacy that she assumed her new client was either a) incredibly lonely, or b) incredibly insecure.

"She's new in town," Dara had said, "so I'm betting it's the first one."

"I'm betting it's neither," Caitlyn had replied, but refused to be drawn into a pleasurable gossip on the subject.

She certainly didn't *look* like a spy, Caitlyn thought, grabbing the mail from Jenny and walking over to her station. Sara was teeny and cute, especially now that Mag's professionals had had their way with her. She was still a brunette, but now her hair was streaked with gold. Her lashes were professionally curled, and her eyes, deep and dark, looked out at the world from beneath professionally plucked brows.

Her pulse and blood pressure no longer skyrocketed whenever Caitlyn walked into the room. She was obviously getting used to these weekly "go-sees," in model parlance.

What a job, Caitlyn thought, not without a twinge

of envy. Go to a salon once a week and keep an eye on the local freak. While you're at it, get your roots done. To think, her tax money paid this woman!

The money. The money . . . Caitlyn tried not to think about the money, but it was difficult. About six days after she'd returned from "neutralizing" Terry, a government check for $16,326.91 had shown up. They had, of course, taken out state and federal taxes, FICA, and something called a CIAA, but there was still plenty left over.

And that was *half* of her check. The Boss had docked her.

She had banked the check—hell, she'd earned it, hadn't she?—and tried very hard to forget that if she just did four or five favors a year for the Boss, she could live very comfortably. It was stupid, because money had never been important to her. Heck, she'd given almost all of hers away, hadn't she? Her dad had held the money over her head so many times, she lost count, and couldn't get rid of it fast enough after the funerals. So she needn't—

Jenny hurried over with a pink message slip, breaking Caitlyn's train of thought. Thank goodness! Worrying about a spy spying on her she completely did not need, as the tiny wrinkles around her eyes would no doubt attest.

"Barb called, says it's an emergency. Home perm," Jenny added in a near whisper. "She's in bad shape. Can you squeeze her in?"

Caitlyn nearly gasped. The horror, the horror! "Sure I can. Poor thing. Tell her to come right over. And *what* was she *thinking*?"

"She let her niece do it for practice," Jenny said over her shoulder. "I guess she didn't think it'd go so bad. Teach her to be nice."

"Boy, no kidding. Agh!" She looked up from brushing off her chair to see Sara standing in front of her. "What do *you* want?"

"The Boss wants to see you," Sara said pleasantly. She smoothed the navy blue smock—every other salon in town did black smocks, *so* eighties—which came down to her knees. "Right away."

"Tell him tough noogies. I've got an emergency."

"You have to cut hair," Sara sniffed.

"Yeah, well, one woman's emergency is another woman's something-or-other."

"I don't think you're hearing me. The Boss wants to see you *now*."

"And I don't think you're hearing *me*, Sara, if that is your real name, which I totally doubt: if you don't get your spying ass out of my face, I'm going to rip your arms off."

Sara backed up. "I don't think—"

"Good-bye."

"—but—"

Caitlyn turned her back on the smaller woman. The Boss wanted to see her now? Tough luck. She had work to do. She had hair, not to mention that most precious of commodities, a woman's self-esteem, to save.

Chapter 12

"I sent for you thirty-eight hours ago," the Boss said. Frothed, actually. He'd been drinking a latte, and foam was sticking to his upper lip. It made him look rabid, which was not an entirely unrealistic image. "What the hell took you so long?"

"I had a hair emergency, then I had to finish my shift, then I had a party."

"You had a *what*?"

"Which word," Caitlyn asked slowly and carefully, "do you need me to define?"

"Party?"

"Why am I not surprised it's *that* word. Okay. A party, noun, is a gathering of friends . . . um. Friend. Okay, let's not get too far ahead of ourselves. A friend is a—"

"You went to a party? The hair thing I *almost* get—you're a small-business owner, you have to please your customers—but a party?"

"It was an important party," she said defensively. "Stacy got her real estate license." Ah, and the beer had flowed, as they said in *Dumb and Dumber,* like wine.

She herself found that she could no longer get drunk—the nanobytes in her system neutralized alcohol like it would any foreign body. Stupid nanobytes! But it had been fun to watch everyone else get silly. One thing about being a cybernetic organism: she was always the designated driver.

She had a sudden vision of herself at age ninety, working her walker and jingling her keys enticingly. "I couldn't not go. Besides, you're not supposed to send for me. We're done, remember?"

"Should have gotten it in writing," the Boss said rudely. "I need you to take care of something for me."

"If it's your nail beds, them I'm your girl. Otherwise, tough shit."

"Never mind my nail beds," he snapped, peeking at his fingers.

Caitlyn folded her cybernetic arms across her chest and sniffed with her cybernetically enhanced nose. "With cuticles like that, I'm not surprised that's your attitude."

"We're getting off the subject. Fine, go to bed with innocent lives on your conscience. Me, I couldn't do that, their dying screams would haunt me for eternity—"

"Don't talk about yourself and a conscience in the same breath unless you want me to die of laughter. And what are you talking about?"

He slid a file across the desk toward her. She didn't touch it, didn't even twitch. "Break it down for me, buddy."

"After all the trouble my secretary went to to

type all this up," he whined. "Very well. One of our agents has gone rogue and is killing people. We don't want him to do that anymore. Is that simple enough for you?"

"Listen to me carefully," she said. "I am a hair jockey. Not a cop. I think just about anyone else in this building, including your secretary, is better qualified to do this job than I am."

"Tough shit. You're up."

"And I'm amazed you're even asking me."

"Then you haven't been paying attention the last few months. Good luck!"

"I didn't mean from the point of view of you should feel shame for bugging me again," she explained through gritted teeth, "although you totally should. I meant you've probably got about fifty more qualified agents to do this and you darn well know it. Not to mention the Minneapolis Police Department."

"As long as you're still here, get me another latte, will you?"

"I can't do it," she said as if speaking to the very young or very stupid. "I wouldn't know where to begin. And don't be stupid on purpose and tell me how to work the foamer."

"*Moi?* Never. And you can begin by reading the file."

"No."

"Uh . . . do it or I'll have you killed?"

"You'd never," she said smugly. "I'm too expensive."

"There are other ways to make you suffer."

"Worse than what's happening right now? The mind reels."

"You know, most people are afraid of me."

Caitlyn yawned.

"So are we still on for tonight, or what?"

"Yes. Although how you can ask that question when you're still hung over from last night is beyond me."

Stacy sat up and stretched, then clutched her head. Caitlyn had driven her home—Stacy was bunking at Casa James while her apartment was being painted from Easy Green to Coral Cockleshells— and had enough time to get Stacy's sandals off before the woman passed out cold. "Hey, it's not every week I sell a house. Well, actually, it apparently *is* every week I sell a house. Ugh, I need a Bloody Mary."

Caitlyn snickered into her coffee cup. "You need a 12-step program."

"Hey, we can't all be—uh—whatever it is you are now. What, you don't get hangovers anymore?"

"I don't get *drunk* anymore."

"Bummer." Stacy said it with convincing sympathy . . . even horror. Then, hopefully, "Is there more coffee?"

"Yup."

"Well, gimme a cup. I'll take it in the shower with me." Stacy shrugged out of her blazer. "Although the thought of those heavy drops of water pounding the shit out of my poor skull is almost more than I can bear."

"You better toss those panty hose," Caitlyn observed, getting up to retrieve the paper. "They're a wash."

"So's this whole outfit."

"Yeah, but I could have told you that last night. A mud brown blazer and a sunshine yellow dress?"

"Natural colors, baby. It's all the rage. Yellow is the new black."

"I thought brown was the new black."

Stacy looked at her pityingly. "Five years ago maybe. Cripes. They need to cybernetically modify your fashion sense, m'girl."

"Look who's talking," she mumbled, sitting down with that morning's edition of the *Trib*. Pure force of habit; if she wanted, she could have the day's stories downloaded directly into her head via the World Wide Web. But frankly, the thought of downloading *anything* directly into her head—her *head!*—was a little creepy.

She stopped when she saw the headline, and nearly sprayed out her coffee. "Oh, shit."

"What?"

"Oh, *shit.*"

"What, I'm dying here, what oh shit?" Stacy hobbled over, clutching her temples, and peeked over Caitlyn's shoulder. " 'TWO MORE FOUND DEAD IN'—what? I mean, it's sad and all, but what's it got to do with—oh."

"I *don't work* for him," she said, almost spat out. "Them. We went over the whole thing. Again. I made it pretty clear. And it was lame that I even had to, I mean, a bionic manicurist is still a manicurist."

"Sure. I mean, you're not the police, right?"

"*Damn* right. And I—I'm not qualified to go after a serial killer. A fucking serial killer! Shit, the *FBI's* barely qualified to go after them. And it's—it's their mess. Not mine."

"Caitlyn, I totally agree with you. It's not your job. You do heads. Let the cops do killers."

"Right."

"Right."

"Shit."

"That too."

Chapter 13

"I'm looking for Caitlyn James," the Boss said. He looked around the busy apartment with interest bordering on alarm. There were, at rough count, about a thousand people crammed into the nine-hundred-square-foot apartment. He'd never seen such a fire hazard in his life. And he'd been *at* fires. The newest Beyoncé CD was on the stereo, and the whir of blenders kept punctuating the air. "I'm her supervisor."

Stacy blinked at the man, who was exactly her height and had the most evil eyes she had ever seen. Also the most expensive suit and the palest eyebrows. She was instantly captivated. "Hi," she said, sticking her hand out. The Boss shook it, then dropped it. "I'm Stacy Gwen."

"Yes, I know. I've seen pictures." He paused, then added somewhat awkwardly, "They don't do you justice."

"Thanks. I think. It's nice of you to come to the party."

"I wasn't exactly invited," he said, weirdly compelled to tell the truth to Stacy Gwen, whose surveillance photos, driver's license photo, and government file did not convey a tenth of the woman's charm.

"Yeah, I know. Which is quite a trick, for one of *these* parties. Um, Caitlyn's around here somewh—"

"Who's this?" Dara cried, bouncing up to them like Tigger after one too many margaritas. "Oooh," she said, fingering the Boss's lapel. "Great suit!"

"This is Caitlyn's new boss. The one she's been, um, talking so much about. The postmaster general of Minnesota."

The Boss rolled his eyes as Dara looked suitably impressed. "Is that like being a military general?" she asked, letting go of the Boss's spotless lapel. "Or is it more like being, like, a civilian?"

"No, and no. I'm here to see Caitlyn." Then, as Dara shrugged and turned away, he said to Stacy, "Postmaster general?"

"Well, you know. She took that civil service exam and all. That was during her 'I'd better have something to fall back on in case Mag doesn't work' phase. And even though *you* said she could tell everybody she's like, Super Alias, *I* don't think it's a good idea."

The Boss took a closer look at Caitlyn's friend. "That was fast thinking."

"Oh, I've had, like, a week to come up with it. It wasn't fast at all." She grinned, showing perfectly straight teeth, the results of an adolescence spent in the heartbreak of braces. She looked good, which was par for the course, and she was just drunk enough to not be intimidated by the guy, who was old enough to be her uncle but dressed way better. "Drink?"

"Yes."

"Okay, well, we got margaritas and margaritas."

"I'll have the latter."

"So, you're here about the dead guys, I bet," Stacy said, shooing three Delta Delta Delta fraternity fellows away from the blenders. "We saw them in the paper this morning. It's okay if we talk about this, right?" she nearly shouted, desperate to be heard over the din.

"It's fine. Nobody's paying any attention to us. And yes, I'm here about the dead guys. We could use your friend's help."

"Oh, dude. That's not why you're here, is it?" Stacy's mussy hair seemed to stand up in horror. "Do you really think that's a good idea? Don't you think you should have, like, a team of *Alias* types on this? Instead of dumping it on Caitlyn?"

"She'll have support," he said defensively. "Thank you." His tongue darted out, snakelike, and licked some of the salt off the rim of his glass. "Don't you think she owes it to her country?"

"Dude, don't get me started, okay?"

"What does that mean?"

"It means drink up." They drank in silence, broken by Stacy after a minute, "So, you're like, the head of this super-secret government agency, huh?"

"Something like that. And you're a real estate agent as of fifteen days ago."

"Yeah, well. So, do you like your job?"

"I love my country," he said robotically.

"Uh-*huh*. Listen, do you want to get out of here?"

"Yes," he said. "But I can't. I have to talk to Caitlyn."

"Well, listen. Take some advice from a gal who has known Caitlyn lo these many years."

He snickered. "Lo?"

"If she sees you here, crashing her party just to bug her about her patriotic duty—so *not* the button to push, BTW—she'll just get her back up. But you know what she spent the day doing?"

"Yes. I'm sure there's a file somewhere."

"Right, well, do you know what it *means*?" Stacy asked patiently. "She spent the day explaining to me, in great and dull detail, why it's not her job to go after your rogue-killer dude. And she explains why she shouldn't do something only when she's just about made up her mind that she's *gonna* do it. So if I were you, I'd just let Caitlyn come to you."

"Mmmm."

"So, I repeat: do you want to get out of here?"

The Boss studied her. "I really shouldn't. It's—it's not like me. And I don't like to leave unless I've gotten what I want."

"Well, maybe you just didn't know what you wanted exactly." Stacy refilled his glass. "You know what I mean?"

"No. Why don't you explain it to me? And may I say, that is a lovely blouse."

"It's the new black, dude."

"So I hear."

"Oh, dude!" Stacy rolled over, tried to find her bra amid the pile of coats, gave up, and flopped back.

"Ditto. That was—"

"Quick. But nice," she added hastily. "Look, I usually ask this question before nudity rears its ugly head, but in all the excitement, I forgot."

"Two hundred thirty thousand a year."

"Not that. But good to know, BTW. What's your name?"

"Uh . . ."

"And don't make something up either, because I have, like, a total sixth sense about this stuff."

"Well, everybody just calls me the Boss," he said cautiously, running his knuckles down her bare arm.

"I *know* that. What's your mama call you?"

"I never had a mother."

"What's the name on your birth certificate?" she asked, exasperated.

"Baby Boy Tyler."

"Oh. Uh, never mind. But damned if I'm going to call you Boss. How about Fred?"

He grinned in the dark. "Do not call me Fred."

"Marty?"

"Pass."

"Bill?"

"Do I look like a Bill?"

"I dunno *what* you look like," she said. "A scary white guy is what I thought. But you're all hype."

"Really?"

"Yeah. Damn, where's my underpants?"

"Under my—there."

"Thanks."

"You're leaving?"

"No, I just like to know where my underwear is. Besides, you did a pretty good job jamming the door closed with Caitlyn's office chair; I don't think anybody's gonna barge in on us." She giggled. "God, she's going to die when I tell her I nailed the Boss."

"I thought I nailed you."

"Dude, we kind of nailed each other. God bless the margarita."

"You're not drunk," he said with total certainty.

"Naw. But I never would have had the guts to even talk to you without one or two of those suckers in me."

"Really? But you're so beautiful."

"Oh. Well, I've been blessed with good skin and great hair," she said in a jaunty shampoo-commercial voice, which made him laugh, "and never mind what Caitlyn says about my roots."

"Seriously. I wouldn't think someone like you would be nervous about talking to anybody."

"Well, I am. But thanks." Then, "Someone like me?"

"Oh, you know. You look like an escapee from a *Glamour* photo shoot, not like a real person. And when you talk to people, you're really good at putting them at ease."

"Well, thanks. You're good at—um—"

"Never mind."

There was a long, comfortable silence, broken by his halting "Gregory. It's Gregory."

"Well, all right. It's better than Marty, God knows."

"That's true." He paused again, then said, "I'd appreciate it if this stayed between us."

"All right, ya weirdo. Uh, listen, Gregory . . ." Now it was her turn to struggle with words. "I . . . I gotta . . . um . . ."

"Oh, dear. You're breaking up with me already?"

She snorted, then wrenched it out. "Thanks for saving my friend, okay? I mean, bottom line, she's alive because of your guys, what you told them to do. And—and I don't know what I would have done, you know?"

"No, I guess I don't know. Not like I know the weight of light or the twenty-ten budget."

"Light has *weight?*" she said, appalled. "That's so lame!"

"No, it's science. Anyway. I don't have any friends," he said, "but I have a vivid imagination. It doesn't sound very nice. So, you're welcome."

"I don't suppose you've figured out where my bra is?"

"It's in my front left pants pocket. I was, uh, planning on taking it home."

"Oh. That's kind of cute. No, creepy. No, cute."

"Thanks," he said dryly.

Chapter 14

Caitlyn wondered where Stacy had disappeared to. Literally disappeared . . . her scans didn't show her anywhere in the building. Maybe her new fella had taken her out for a late cup of coffee or something. Which fella? Had she decided between Mark and Tim? Caitlyn figured her cybernetic enhancements would be put to good use just keeping Stacy's love life straight. That lucky bitch.

Of course, with those big brown eyes, Stacy just had to bat her eyelashes at some poor schlub and he followed her anywhere.

Caitlyn sighed. It was enough to make a girl want to poison her best friend's ice supply. Sometimes.

The party was winding down, which was just as well since she had to be at Mag at nine A.M. tomorrow. Later today, actually. Which was fine with her—she set the schedule.

"Caitlyn James?"

"Yeah?" She looked . . . and nearly fell off the

kitchen chair. The best-looking guy in the entire world was in her apartment—her kitchen, actually—scowling at her.

He was tall—seventy-six inches, her chip reported helpfully—and two hundred ten pounds, not a bit of it flab. He had the blackest hair she'd ever seen, and blue eyes that put Terrance-the-former-virgin to shame . . . they were the color of the Caribbean on a cloudless day. She'd never seen eyes that color before unless colored contacts were involved.

He had a strong jaw that bloomed with dark stubble, and broad shoulders set off splendidly by the black greatcoat he wore.

"You work for the O.S.F.?"

She forced her mouth, which had popped open, to form the word no.

His scowl deepened, if that was possible. Instead of scaring her, it made her horny. Terrance had been fast but not terribly skilled. Not skilled at all, frankly. Well, it was understandable . . . poor fellow spent all his time writing code, and zero time trying to get laid. But this guy. *This* guy looked like he knew what he was doing. Regarding everything.

"Oh. Then my information is incorrect."

She blinked. "Okay."

"Good-bye."

"Bye. Thanks for coming."

Okay, she thought as he swept out of her apartment, the greatcoat flapping behind him like some black bird of prey. *That was weird. Question is, what am I going to do about it?*

Nothing. If the O.S.F. wanted to send some gorgeous weirdo to her apartment, but then he had the good manners to leave, she wasn't going to do anything about it. Was she? No.

Er, why?

Because she couldn't. That would be admitting she worked for those conscienceless bastards.

But oh, she could dream. . . .

Chapter 15

The Boss entered the building at 5:32 A.M. and skimmed some files on the elevator ride to his office. Since he knew ahead of time what the *Trib* and the *Pioneer Press* would print, it was a waste of time to read the paper.

"Caitlyn James is waiting for you," Rebecca told him as he entered. In the six years she had been his assistant, he had never beaten her to the office. He swore she had his car bugged. "And there's a hearing at two P.M."

"Great. And great. Please order ten dozen roses, assorted colors, and have them sent here." He handed her Stacy's card.

Rebecca's mouth popped open. "Uh—sure. Sure. Right away. I'll use the florist we—sure." He watched, amused, as she pretended her boss had her send flowers to women every day. "Alrighty, then. Does that have anything to do with why you're wearing yesterday's Armani?"

"That's classified, Rebecca."

"Sure it is," she snickered.

"How long has Caitlyn been waiting?"

"Forty minutes."

"Great. Order a replacement of everything."

"Already done."

He opened his door—miraculously still hanging by the hinges—and observed the six-billion-dollar woman had twisted around in her chair and was looking decidedly sullen. "Finally," she said by way of greeting.

"Good morning."

"Okay, first of all, don't crash my parties."

"Fine, thanks, and you?"

"And second of all, don't send other creeps to crash my parties either. And third of all, you having an out-of-control agent is not my problem, but I'm gonna look into it anyway. This does *not* mean I'm working for you. I'm just curious myself, okay?"

"No, I don't think it will rain, but I wish it would, we could certainly use it."

"Fourth, your coffee sucks."

He sat down and thought about Stacy's smile, which nicely offset her gorgeous dark eyes, her big, beautiful brown eyes with that charming tilt at the corners, then shoved Stacy out of his mind and focused on the matter at hand. "I've prepared a file for you—"

"By 'I've' you mean 'my assistant,' right?"

"Yes." Odd. Stacy was back. He had banished her as he had banished every distraction for the last—er, how old was he?—and she was back. Was ten dozen enough? Perhaps he should double the flower order. It wouldn't do to appear lacking. Not to a woman like that. She probably had a dozen men battling for her favors. "Take the plane to Paris."

"Paris?" Caitlyn looked surprised and pleased, so he decided, cruelly, to let her be even more surprised when she got off the plane. "Oh! Okay. Well, I'd better get going."

"Yes, you had better." Odd. He had won, and all he could think about was this: were ten dozen flowers enough? "It was a lovely party, BTW."

"What?" She looked alarmed and suspicious—and ridiculous, with black streaks in her white blond hair. He was positive that the last time he'd seen her the streaks had been red.

"Nothing." He turned to the computer, fired off a quick two-word e-mail to Rebecca ("Twenty dozen"), then turned back to Caitlyn. "Were you aware that brown is the new black?"

His six-billion-dollar project rolled her eyes, which were the color of the deep end of a pool. "I told you not to come to my parties anymore, right?"

"Yes." The problem with science for science's sake—which was ninety-five percent of the reason O.S.F. was funded—was that the scientists insisted on inventing things. Like nanobytes. Then they wanted to skip animal testing—and, needless to say, testing on federal prisoners—and go right to cleancut Americans.

"Don't worry." Then, when an experiment actually worked, *he* had to find a use for it. Thus, a former sorority girl and current barber was now on his payroll. If he thought about it too long, he might laugh. Stranger things had happened. "I got what I needed last night."

"Because I really, really need for you to get that."

"Yes, yes, I'll never do it again." He had always thought of Caitlyn's fine good looks as an asset to O.S.F., but if she kept doing odd things to her hair, he was going to have to send her a memo. "Be sure to read the file, Caitlyn." If past performance had been any indicator, he knew the more he emphasized something, the higher the probability that she would do the opposite.

She was a child, really. A beautiful child, but lacking in discipline and deportment. Now, Stacy was young, but she was charming and quite mature for her years, really had a grasp of—

"I think I may be in rather large trouble," he announced.

"Dude, you're only now figuring that out? You're kidnapping women and infecting them with nanobytes, you've got a rogue agent killing people, and you're crashing parties because you have no life."

"Don't call me dude," he said. That was what Stacy called him. It was, like, her pet name for him. Had he just used "like" as an adjective?

"How about if I call you jackass?"

"How about if you go away and let me work?"

Caitlyn huffed out. Engrossed in paperwork, he didn't even watch her go.

Chapter 16

Caitlyn finished the last paper airplane and sailed it across the cabin. Now the file was empty. Hee!

Okay, so, she'd have to read some of it to find out where the bad guy was, but she'd do that when they landed and the Spy Car was driving her wherever she needed to go. Hell, the Spy Car would probably take her to the bad guy, most likely. Then she'd neutralize him or whatever. She'd worry about that later, but one thing was for sure. She had to get that done before she shopped.

Not that she wasn't dying to shop. Because she absolutely was. But if she shopped, all the ghosts of the people the bad guy had killed would just bother the hell out of her. So she'd get work out of the way, then enjoy her first-ever trip to Paris.

The copilot opened the door to the cockpit and stuck his head into the cabin. "Ma'am, we're landing."

She peeked out the window. "Already?"

"Yes, ma'am. Buckle up."

"I'm buckled." She looked out the window again and opened her mouth, but the copilot had ducked back inside the cockpit. "Well, shoot."

She waited until they had landed and taxied, out of force of habit—though it would probably take a lot more than a plane crash to ice her—then unbuckled and stood. The copilot had come out again and gallantly held out a hand to help her out of her seat.

"Thanks."

"No problem. We're here, ma'am."

"Uh, hello? I think you guys need to get new maps, pronto."

"Paris, Texas."

"Aw, shit."

"And the Boss said to tell you it serves you right for not reading the file."

"Aw, shit!"

"That's why I had to plow through two hundred paper airplanes to get my coffee, isn't it?"

"I hate him," she said, looking out her window at the barren expanse that was the Paris, Texas, airport, "so much."

"We all do, ma'am."

"So the Waldorf . . . ?"

"It's the Wally Dorfman Motel. See, Wally's the mayor, and he owns the place on the side, and—"

"I actually have no interest in this at all."

"Oh."

"There's a car out there, right?"

"Yes, ma'am."

"It's Caitlyn, okay? Stop with the ma'am. And the car is going to whisk me away somewhere."

"Yes, ma'am."

"So I don't actually need to read the file," she finished triumphantly.

"If you say so, ma'am."

"Oh, I say so. Thanks for the ride."

She slouched down the steps to the tarmac, shamelessly eavesdropping on the pilot and copilot's conversation.

"She's a field agent, right?"

"Yeah, but she's new."

"Really new if she's not reading the file."

"Yeah, but, God, wouldn't you like to tear a piece off of—"

Caitlyn stopped listening. On the tarmac below, waiting for her, was the same driver she had last time.

"Oh, it's you," she said. The chip in her head obediently played back the conversation where the woman had told Caitlyn her name. "Sharon, right? Nice to see you again."

Sharon smiled at her, and the wind ruffled her hair. Prematurely gray, Caitlyn thought. She needs a good rinse to cover it. Maybe Light Auburn #421. "Hi, Caitlyn. Well, here we go again. You gonna actually shoot this one?"

"Probably not."

"Have it your way." Sharon snickered as she held the door open. "We're off to the Waldorf."

"Oh, if only."

". . . then I'm supposed to meet with this detective guy, Detective Johnson, and get the scoop from him, and then I guess I'll use my incredible new brain to crack the case. I foresee nothing going wrong with this plan. At all."

Sharon snickered. "I thought you didn't read files. You're sort of famous for it."

"Well, I kind of scanned the papers before I made them into airplanes. It's all up here." She tapped her temple. "I just haven't looked at it yet."

"You can download information without knowing exactly what it is?"

"Sure. Like e-mail, I guess. You know, when you're downloading something and you don't know what it is. Good way to get a virus actually," she added in a mutter.

"Hmf."

"Sharon, we have to talk about this way you have of grunting instead of speaking."

"No, we have to get to work," Sharon said, pulling up outside the motel, which was painted a depressing shade of brown. "Luck."

"What could possibly go wrong?" she asked glumly, slamming the car door. To punctuate her mood, it started to rain. This was apparently a rare and wonderful thing in Paris, Texas, but it was pretty damned common in Minneapolis, aka the Seattle of the Midwest.

She stomped through the lobby—no need to mess with the front desk, since the key to her room had been in the file—and down the hall to her room, popped the door open, and slung her purse on the small table in the breakfast nook.

ALARM ALARM ALARM ALARM ALARM
ALARM AL

Too late, she realized she should have scanned the room for life signs. Well, she'd said, hadn't she? *She was not cut out for this job.*

She heard a sound, but there was no pain. Instead, she watched the screen in her head fade to black, exactly like a television set.

So that's what losing consciousness feels like, she thought, tipping sideways. *It's so, er, what's the word? It's on the tip of my tongue. Great, now I can't think of it. Detached! No, that's not it. Anyway, it's very int—*

Chapter 17

"Owwwwwww," she complained, sitting up and rubbing the back of her neck. "What did you hit me with, a taxi?"

"No," her attacker said coolly. He followed it up with, "You're not what I expected at all."

She saw who it was and leapt from the bed. Truth be told, her neck didn't hurt that much. Okay, not at all. But she kept rubbing it anyway, hoping for a sympathetic look. Or sympathetic oral sex.

"You! The guy from my party!"

The guy from her party frowned at her. Okay, so now she knew he had two expressions: a frown and a scowl. Progress! "First you crash my party, and now this? Oh, you're gonna pay, pal. Through the *nose*."

"We have to talk," he said.

"Dude, I have to kick your ass! And then haul you to jail! Or kill you! I haven't decided which! Am I shouting? It seems kind of loud in here."

"Yes, you're shouting. Now lie back down on the

bed before you hurt yourself." He tried to put his hands on her shoulders, and she shrugged him off.

"I'll pass." She rubbed her arms and grimaced. "I saw this TV special once on hotel rooms and how they, like, never wash the bedspreads, and let's just say, my skin is crawling just standing on this carpet."

He glared at her with his gorgeous blue eyes. He had retreated from the bed and was now standing directly in front of the door, so the first thing a visitor would smack into would be his back. Unless, of course, he punched them from behind, or whatever he did. She stifled a sigh as he said, "Let's try to stay on track, shall we?"

"Okay. Let's talk about how you creepily waited in my room and then clobbered me when I wasn't looking."

"I didn't clobber you."

"You did something!"

"It doesn't matter."

"Pal: What. Did. You. Do."

He said calmly, which was infuriating enough, "There's a—a reboot spot, I suppose you could call it. It's on the back of your neck. If someone applies just the right amount of pressure—"

"I'll . . . what? Turn off?" She found the thought as appalling as she did horrifying. Nobody—*nobody*—at the O.S.F. had mentioned this little tidbit. *"You turned me off?"*

"More like shut you down for a minute. It's painless and leaves no lasting damage."

"I've got an off switch?"

"You're shouting again," he pointed out helpfully.

"Ugh! Ugh-ugh! And again, ugh!" She didn't know what was worse, finding out she could be shut off by someone who knew what she was, or that he was so matter-of-fact about it. "Jesus Christ!"

"Let's talk about the O.S.F."

"Fuck a duck!"

"You lied," he continued, inexorable as a Terminator.

That got her attention. She was a weird-ass cyborg freak with an off switch, but she was *not* a liar. "I never!"

"You said you didn't work for them."

"I *don't.* It was just a one-time thing. I'm just here because—actually, it's a really long story and there's, like, no alcohol in this room, so I'm not gonna tell it. Not even if you say pretty please with sugar on top. So there!"

He blinked at her. She had the odd feeling that he was doing more than looking at her leggings and shirt. Then she realized: he was scanning her! Just like she did pretty much automatically these days; she recognized the look, penetrating and faraway at the same time. But that would mean—

She scanned *him* (Ha! See how he likes it!) and got exactly what she had gotten last time: his yummy measurements, but little else.

"You'd better not have X-ray vision, or if you do, you'd better not be using it."

He didn't say anything.

"I don't get it."

"Now, if only you had a ten-dollar bill for every time you've had to say that out loud."

"Hey, there's no need to be mean. Are you"— she hesitated—"like me?"

"No."

"Oh, c'mon, seriously."

"No one is like you, I think."

"Okay, thanks, I think."

"Am I cybernetically enhanced?" he prompted her.

"Who are you talking to?" she asked.

He frowned again. "The answer is yes."

"But—" But the Boss had told her she was the only one. Gosh, the evilest man in the universe had lied to her, what a large fucking surprise. "But—" But if he was like her, that would mean—

"But when I scan you, I don't pick up anything unusual."

"That's because I can block your scans."

She digested that for a minute, then asked, "So, you work for the O.S.F.?"

His frown deepened and his eyes went all narrow and squinty. He was either constipated or super pissed.

"Okay, okay," she said nervously. "Don't have a stroke."

"I *never* worked for Gregory Hamlin," he said in a low voice that was nonetheless the most vehement tone she had ever heard. "I never worked for any of them. I was a slave."

"Okay, okay, I believe you. Uh, who?"

"He's about your height, slicked-back hair, everybody calls him the Boss?"

"Oh, him. Well, me neither. Yeah! We're two lone wolves alone, er, together. Just you and me against the world, pal." Now, why was that thought as horrifying as it was exciting?

"Mmmm. Now, I know better than anyone how infuriating it is to be turned into something new against your will, but you simply must stop killing the members of the Wagner team to get your point across."

She gaped at him. Well, she felt like doing that anyway. He was wearing a crisp white shirt, a blue tie the exact color of his eyes, and black slacks. Ymmm. Oh, and probably shoes and socks, but frankly, she hadn't been able to bring her gaze past his waist. He could be wearing pink rubber flip-flops for all she cared. "I've got to what to get my what and stop doing *what?*"

"This dumb act you're putting on is really quite good, but it's wasted on me. So—"

Finally, she got it. Normally, she wasn't this slow, but it had been an odd day, and not even lunchtime yet. "*I'm* not the killer! *You're* the killer!"

"Stop yelling."

"I'm not yelling! It's totally you! I just don't know why," she confessed. "But it doesn't matter, because I've got to bring you in." *I guess. How does one bring in a suspect exactly? I know! I'll wear him out having sex with him. No, wait, that's a dumb idea. Or is it a great idea?*

"I'm not the one murdering all those people," he said impatiently. "You are."

She laughed shortly. "Pal, I think I would know if I was going around killing people."

"Look. I already told you, I understand. So if you'll just—"

"Wait a minute. You understand? So . . . what? You're going to arrest me and take me in, or whatever?"

"No. What jail could hold you, first of all?"

She buffed her nails on her shirt. "Well, that's true."

"And your position . . . it's understandable. Not that I condone murder," he said, fixing her with a frown, "or, not usually."

"Well, color me comforted."

"But I understand how you feel. I just think there are other ways to, ah, get your point across."

"So, what d'you want to do?"

"I'll take you into my custody, and there are people in my employ who can help you."

"Uh-huh. And you're doing this why?"

He blinked. "Because it's wrong to go around killing people, as you put it. No matter what they did to deserve it."

"Uh-*huh*. So I go with you and you help me and nobody else gets murdered and everybody's happy except the Boss, who will probably swallow all his teeth when I call to tell him that I'm with—okay. I'm in."

Chapter 18

There were a few flaws in her plan, she thought, staring dreamily at what's-his-name's hands as he shifted gears. He had wonderful hands, big and blocky, and the knuckles were sprinkled with fine black hair. If she couldn't stare into his dreamy blue eyes, she'd stare at his hands. Oh, and think about the flaws. Right. That too.

Flaw number one: she wasn't the killer.

Flaw number two: she wasn't sure he was, but on the chance that he wasn't, the killer was still running around loose. Killing . . . what did he say? Members of the Wagner team? She knew about them, they were the team that had infected her. Wagner for Jamie Wagner, the Bionic Woman. Ha. Ha. Ha. Somebody at the O.S.F. was watching too many reruns.

Flaw number three: she had just agreed to be taken into what's-his-name's custody for an indefinite amount of time.

Flaw number four: she didn't know what's-his-name's name.

Flaw number five: she was letting her hormones do her thinking for her, which, while almost always resulting in short-term satisfaction, led to long-term poor results.

Flaw number six: the Boss.

"That reminds me," she said. "I need to make a phone call."

"Where's your cell phone?"

"Pal, you're probably looking at the one person in the state of Minnesota who doesn't have one."

"*Gregory Hamlin sent a green recruit into the field without a cell phone?*"

"Don't yell. I'm sitting right here."

"Unbelievable," what's-his-name muttered. "Truly. The mind reels. The mind is boggled."

"Pal." She snapped her fingers. "Are you with me? Stay focused, okay? I. Need. A. Phone."

"When we get to the jet, you can use mine."

"Okay." Jet? Oooh. Jet? "Jet?"

"Yes."

"Where are we going?"

"My home."

"Okey-dokey."

She supposed it was time she read that stupid file. She settled back in the luxurious leather seats of the whatever it was he was driving—she had never been a car babe—and closed her eyes. And read.

Dmitri Novakov sneaked another glance at the odd blonde in the seat next to him and nearly drove into a telephone pole. That's enough of that, he told himself. Pay attention. Yes, she's quite pretty, but that's also quite irrelevant.

He had calculated several results from his trip to the motel, but the probability of her willingly going with him was only eight point five two three percent. The probability that he would have had to kill her had been almost sixty percent. He was, frankly, amazed she'd gotten into his Lexus.

He would have to redo all his calculations, because as it was, he was playing it by ear. And he *hated* playing it by ear. Too many variables made it impossible to predict outcome with any accuracy.

And now . . . she was asleep!

He quickly calculated the probability of the Wagner team killer agreeing to come with him and then falling asleep in his car. It was low . . . one point two six seven percent.

It was all very strange, and she was possibly the strangest of all in what he knew to be a very odd and cutthroat business. For a field agent, she was remarkably . . . real.

Of course, they trained them to be charming, and pretty girls were often specifically recruited, but truly, she was like no other woman he had met. And the amazing thing was, it had nothing to do with the fact that she was the *other* cybernetically enhanced human being walking around on the planet.

No, it was just her. When she wasn't yelling, she was . . . well, yelling. But when she'd regained consciousness, she had been more angry than scared. In fact, he didn't believe she had been scared at all.

Most agents, upon waking in the presence of

the Wolf, would have soiled themselves in terror.
Or at least cringed a little. Not this one. Not this . . .
Caitlyn.

And what could her sinister motive be, to willingly come with him? Was he on her hit list? It
would make sense, of a twisted sort . . . she had certainly taken care of enough of the Wagner team.

That was perhaps the oddest thing of all. She
didn't seem like a cold, detached assassin. She was
more like . . . like someone you might run into at a
coffee shop.

But perhaps that was part of her skill.

Chapter 19

"Caitlyn James is coming in on the SAT line," Rebecca told the Boss. "And the senator from Florida canceled."

"Good. And good. Now I don't have to cancel on him. Patch Caitlyn through. Oh, and have one of the boys bring my car around. I'm leaving at five."

Rebecca's jaw dropped, and she backed out of the room as if unsure if he would leap over the desk and strangle her.

The Boss rolled his eyes. Okay, so he was married to his job. And he seldom left the office before nine P.M. (Frankly, he didn't know how bankers and brokers pulled off that whole forty-hour-work-week thing.) But was it so terrifically unusual that he wanted to leave at a decent hour in order to take Stacy to the Oceanaire? Not at all. But meet a nice girl and send her flowers and take her to dinner and you'd think it was one of the signs of the Apocalypse.

He picked up the SAT line. "Mirage, this is Team Leader. Go."

"What?" Caitlyn said. The connection was excellent; it sounded, unfortunately, like she was in the room with him.

"Mirage. That's your code name when you're in the field," he explained, "and I'm Team Leader. This is an SAT line, which means—"

"Yeah, yeah, save it for the technogeeks. Why Mirage?"

"Because, frankly, nobody here ever knows when you'll show up for a mission. You've only yourself to blame for that one. *Mirage.*"

"I hate you. And it's not a simple, easy hate like people hating fish. I hate you like the plague. I hate you like a famine. I—"

"Mirage, can we speed this up? You have no idea what this is costing me per minute."

"Aw, go bitch to AT&T. Listen, there were just a few tiny details you forgot to share with me when you sent me to Paris. Paris, *Texas,* you big jerkoff."

He giggled. He couldn't help it. "Describe exactly what your face looked like when you found out you weren't in the City of Light. Leave out nothing."

"How about I describe what *your* face is gonna look like after I get done pounding it for about three hours? Now listen to me, you sadistic fuck. You didn't tell me the guy you think is killing all the geeks is not only *not* a former agent of yours, but he's been infected with nanobytes too!"

"It was all in the file," he said inexorably. Sadistic fuck? Lord, the mouth on this girl. He peeked at his watch. He'd finish up this call and then go pick Stacy up. He should probably give his bodyguards the night off. They might cramp Stacy's style. "Every bit of it."

"Dmitri Novakov . . . The Wolf? Hello, could he have a scarier code name? Why not just call him Killer and be done with it?"

"We can't all get Mirage," he said with a straight face.

She ignored his obvious jibe and proceeded to tell him things he already knew. He yawned and peeked at his watch while she droned on. "Lithuanian by birth, nationalized here when he was twenty-two. Speaks flawless English, Russian, Japanese, French, and Spanish? Oh, and did I mention, he's a freak like me?"

"No one is a freak like you. That is both your blessing and your curse." *Not to mention mine.*

"Oh, save it for the recruiting speech, ya big weirdo. Plus . . . plus! I recognized one of the dead guys. Which gave me a total start, I can tell you. He was Egghead #1. He's the guy who was hanging around when I woke up in the hospital after you ruined my life."

"Yes, Dr. Jeeter."

"Jeeter? Like Skeeter? Look, all I know is, he was one of your main dudes for the nanoteam, and he's dead. Along with two of his team members."

"Mirage," he said, forcing patience, "*I* know all this."

"Well, thanks for mentioning it! Bad enough I had to spend almost two hours in Texas—do you know what that climate did to my ends?"

"Your what?"

"My *ends*, the ends of *my hair.* Next time send me to Ireland. I read somewhere that all the moisture in the air is great for your skin. But I digress."

"Yes," he agreed, resting his forehead on his hand. He had his daily Caitlyn headache, right on time. Never mind a Tylenol. He needed a jab of morphine.

"Bad enough I even set foot on that lame plane of yours to go *anywhere*. Bad enough you send me after a guy you so affectionately named the Wolf. But you think he's killing the team that made him? And me?"

"Well," the Boss said reasonably, "someone is."

"And he thinks it's me!"

"Don't be ridiculous. If it was you, we'd know."

"Well, thanks for that. I think. Plus, he says he never worked for you."

"Well, he's wrong," the Boss snapped.

"So, he worked for you like *I* work for you, which is to say not at all, you lame, delusional weirdo. That is, you think we're working for you, but in our hearts we're not."

"Oh, Caitlyn, you've really got to jettison this idea of personal freedom you—wait a minute. He *said*? You've spoken to the Wolf?"

"Dude, I'm in his plane right now!"

The Boss nearly dropped the phone. How vastly he had underestimated Caitlyn James! She had left his office that morning and, in the hours that followed, tracked down the Wolf (the Wolf!), took him into custody, and commandeered his private jet. Now she was returning to him in triumph. Oh, it was sweet.

"Mirage . . . I don't know what to say. I'm very p—"

"If you say you're proud of me, I'm barfing right into the phone, you wretch."

"I was going to say I'm very pleased," he lied.

"Well, don't sprain your elbow patting yourself on the back, chum. I think you might be jumping to a few conclusions. He's not with me. I'm with him."

"What?"

"You heard me. We got to talking in the Wally Dorfman Motel . . . something else I'll be kicking your ass for now that I think of it, and anyway, I'm going home with him."

His knuckles whitened on the phone. "Is this . . . is this part of your plan?"

"My plan to get laid, maybe." She laughed. "Don't wait up . . . Boss."

There was a gentle click as she hung up. But even though she was thousands of miles away, flying over the ocean somewhere, he could still hear her laughing.

Chapter 20

From the private case files of Dr. Elena Balta

First interview with subject Caitlyn James, 04/18, 14:25 hours. Subject is 24 yo Caucasian female who appears younger than her stated age. Very attractive, well nourished, socks match, coordinated outfit.

Subject was initially given MMPI and Rorschach, scoring above average normal, but has an interesting way of seeing the Boss in most of the inkblots (e.g., "That's that crumb, the Boss, sending me on another assignment. And that's him telling me he's got the receipt. And that's the schmuck telling me I owe the government because they saved my ass, not that I asked them to. And that's—"). Full test scores and interpretations can be found in Appendix A.

Subject is oriented to time and place, seems very interested in her surroundings, and appears in no hurry to return to her home. Subject has asked for the use of a telephone and has called someone named Stacy and someone named Jennifer (full transcripts of conversations can be found in Appendix B).

A brief case history was taken before testing began. Subject's parents are both deceased, killed in a car accident when subject was a teenager. Subject graduated high school and has a bachelor's degree in applied business, and currently styles hair at an American salon in Minnesota, Magnifique.

Subject was part of the Wagner team following a severe car accident and, according to files downloaded from the O.S.F. database, is cybernetically enhanced.

Begin session number one.

"So, am I a slavering sociopath, or what?"

"You tested high normal," Dr. Balta explained. "This is to your credit, and congratulations. However, I feel obliged to tell you that masking responses is an indicator of the sociopathic personality."

"So, what you're saying is, the fact that I tested normal is an ominous development." Caitlyn snickered. "That's like saying the fact that there are no developments is an ominous development."

There was a short silence, then Dr. Balta—who wasn't a bad-looking woman for someone who wouldn't see fifty again—said, "You don't have to lie on the couch, you know. You can sit on one of the chairs."

"No, no, let's get this over with. Jeez, Dmitri didn't waste any time, did he? Hustled me off the plane, to his *castle* no less, and then brought me right to you. A castle. Hello? Am I the only one who feels trapped in an old movie?"

There was another short pause, followed by "Everyone here wants to help you."

"Gosh, that makes me feel so warm and tingly inside . . . okay, it doesn't, really, in fact it kind of creeps me out. So, he keeps his own private shrink in his own private castle?"

"Yes."

"You know, you've got great skin."

"Thank you."

"I bet you never spent a minute in Texas," she continued gloomily.

"No, I've never had that pleasure. I have lived most of my life here. I went to school in Massachusetts but then came back home."

"Uh-huh. And where is 'here'? I asked Dmitri, but he was on the phones—the guy carries two cell phones with him, you believe that?"

"Three," Dr. Balta said.

"And he didn't answer me."

"I apologize. He gets . . . preoccupied . . . at times. Of course you should know where you are. I confess, I was unaware you did not know, and I'm surprised you haven't asked earlier."

"Oh, well." Caitlyn shrugged. "It didn't really matter. What matters is I got to call the jerk and tell him what was going on."

"Mm-hmm. So what you're saying is, the destination did not matter so long as you got your phone call with the j—er, the Boss?"

"Exactly."

"Well, you're in Lithuania."

"Help me out here. We're how many miles from Paris? Paris, *France*?" she added hastily.

"Lithuania is in Eastern Europe," Dr. Balta explained gently. "On the coast of the Baltic Sea. Not very close to Paris."

"Dammit. Okay. Thanks for telling me." She looked around the large office, tastefully decorated in circus clown. "So! You work for the Wolf, huh?"

"Yes."

"Do you like it?"

"As a matter of fact, yes, but, Miss James, we're talking about you."

"Okay, okay, don't get your doctorate in a knot. So you went to school in the States? Because your English is excellent. Better than mine!"

"Thank you. Shall we get down to business?"

"Not very shrinky of you. You're supposed to let me babble on about whatever, and then decide I secretly hated my mother when I was six."

"If I let you babble on about whatever, I will doubtless hear more than I ever wanted to about current American hairstyles."

"Meow! Fine, I suppose you want to talk about all the dead guys. Poor bastards."

"Well. That is why Dmitri brought you here. He's very worried about you. As are we all," she added.

"Uh-huh. Well, set your mind at ease, Dr. Balta. I'm not a slobbering psycho. I never killed anybody. Though I've been tempted. Especially recently."

"Tell me about that," Dr. Balta suggested.

"Oh, this dick who heads up this government team who saved me and then wrecked me. He bugs the hell out of me. I mean, I thought my econ prof was bad. But this guy. He's the worst."

"This would be the man referred to as the Boss?"

"That's him. Except he's not *my* boss."

"Mmm."

"And did you have to show me so many pictures of him? Cripes. I'm trying to digest my lunch here."

Dr. Balta blinked but, to Caitlyn's disappointment, didn't give her Rorschach 101. "So sorry. So you're saying you are not responsible for the murders of the Wagner team?"

"That's right. T'warn't me!" she said cheerfully. "But I'm wondering if it was the Wolf."

"I can assure you, it wasn't."

"Says the loyal, possibly brainwashed employee."

"I've known him his entire life. He will kill, if necessary, to save himself or someone else, but he won't kill for vengeance. It's not . . . logical, I suppose you would say."

"Also, it's morally wrong," Caitlyn prompted.

"Well, yes."

"Gee, I feel much better. Case closed. Back to America! Well, maybe not. I've never been in an honest-to-God castle before."

"It's been in Dmitri's family for three hundred years."

"A real fixer-upper, huh? I couldn't help but notice the lack of central heating. Place is about as warm and cozy as a meat freezer. So, you seem to know a lot about this guy. He hire you when he was four?"

Dr. Balta smiled. "No. He's my son."

"Oh. Whoa!" But she could see it now. They both had the same clear blue eyes and the same dark hair, except Dr. Balta's was sprinkled with silver strands and twisted up in a knot, while the Wolf's was cut brutally short. "That whole different-last-name thing threw me off."

"I remarried after the death of Dmitri's father. But we were talking about you."

"No, we were talking about your kid, and you were explaining that he wouldn't kill all those guys because it's not logical. Now, I don't want to think someone as yummy as your son is responsible for a killing spree, but who else would do it?"

"Besides you," Dr. Balta prompted.

"Well, yeah. Except, I know I didn't do it."

"You seem very angry with the O.S.F. You claim they ruined your life."

"Well, yeah. But I wouldn't, like, *kill* the egghead team. They were just following orders . . . I guess. Buncha dorks."

"The Boss's orders."

"Well, yeah. *Him* I wouldn't mind killing. Except, I can prove I haven't because he's still alive. Ta-dah!"

"Good work," Dr. Balta said, looking more confused by the second.

"Which brings us back to your son."

"Er . . . what?"

"You know, I was told I was the only cybernetically enhanced person on the planet."

"Really?"

"Actually, what he said was 'You are the first of your kind, a fully functioning cybernetic organism who has retained your humanity.' Except that's not true, right? Because there's Dmitri."

"Yes."

"Maybe the Boss meant that Dmitri hadn't retained his humanity?"

Nothing from Dr. Balta.

"Because that would be kind of an interesting, what do you call it . . . observation. Right?"

Silence.

"Helloooooooo?"

"Why would you think that?" she asked at last.

"I dunno. He seemed like kind of a cold one to me."

"Not everyone has your gifts, Caitlyn."

"Gifts? Me? Really? Cool. But don't distract me with flattery. It works, but only for a few seconds."

"I apologize," Dr. Balta said, smothering a smile.

"So, what happened to him? Are you allowed to tell me?"

"Yes. Dmitri has instructed me to answer any of your questions."

"Instructs his mom, huh?"

"He does sign my paycheck," Dr. Balta pointed out.

"So, you have to answer all my questions? That would have been nice to know an hour ago."

"And in response, I can tell you—"

"That he's six foot four, with the blackest hair and the bluest eyes? And totally strapping and yummy? Even if he's chilly and distant? It's all right though. He can ride that whole 'phenomenal good looks' thing for years if he needs to."

"I was going to say, he was infected with nanobytes during a Russian/American cooperative venture . . . this was right after the Berlin Wall was taken down. He was sent in to defuse a bomb and, unfortunately, didn't get clear fast enough. The resulting injuries were . . . massive."

"Oh. Uh, you don't have to talk about it if you don't want to."

"It happened years ago," Dr. Balta said, expressionless, which wasn't exactly the same thing as "Aw, no biggie, I don't mind." "Like you, he resented what had been done to him in the name of science, went rogue, and then the project fell apart. However, it was revived by the man you know as the Boss, just last year. They didn't have to wait very long before you came along, no?"

"No," she said glumly. "Poor Dmitri. Believe me, I know *exactly* how he feels. The Boss is lucky the Wolf didn't pop his head off his neck like a boil."

"I have had thoughts in that direction myself," Dr. Balta admitted.

"Popping the head off? Or being glad your kid didn't do it?"

"We're getting off the topic."

"So what?"

"I have nothing to say in response to that," Dr. Balta admitted.

"Let me sum up the problem for the studio audience. Dmitri thinks I'm the killer. And much as I like his broad, broad shoulders, I can't entirely rule him out either. So, what do we do now? And by we I mean me, of course."

"Perhaps we should take a break," Dr. Balta said.

"Okay." Privately, Caitlyn thought, *If someone else on the Wagner team turns up dead, then he'll know it wasn't me, and I'll know it wasn't him. But if nobody else dies, that doesn't prove anything. Shit.* "Yeah, let's do that."

End session number one.

Chapter 21

"What's the matter?" Stacy asked. "You haven't touched your Rusty Nail. Although it's beyond me how anyone can smell one, much less drink one." She tapped her margarita glass. "Take it from me: if you don't need a blender to make a drink, it ain't a drink."

"It's . . . work. I apologize." The Boss forced a smile. "I had been . . . um . . . looking forward to this evening. I don't mean to . . . uh . . . what's the colloquialism? Bring you down?"

"More like harsh my buzz. Don't worry about it. Hey, if you're having a bad day, we can bag the date. There's always the weekend."

"No, no. I enjoyed our time together last night and wanted to see you again."

Stacy smiled at that. "Awww. You say the sweetest things. I, too, enjoyed our frantic anonymous sex."

The Boss laughed out loud. "Stacy, for the love of—"

"Is it something you can tell me about?"

There was a long pause, followed by "It's Caitlyn."

The smile dropped away. "Oh. Well, good luck with *that*."

"Yes, I imagine you don't want to get in the middle. Unless . . ." His eyes narrowed suspiciously. "That's not why you're here, is it? To perhaps influence my handling of your friend?"

"Influence your handling? Ewwwww! God, I'm gonna need five more 'ritas just to get that mental picture out of my head."

The Boss smiled. "I apologize."

"Seriously, don't do that! Yech. Besides, I'm here because I'm hoping to get more good lovin', like last night."

"Oh."

"So there it is."

"All right."

"Also, I really like your suit. Do you have, like, fifty of them at home?"

"Trade secret."

"Uh-huh." She peered at him, then took a bite of her flounder and another sip of her drink. "Frankly, I don't know what it is. You could not be less my type."

"Too old?"

"Too white, pal. But there's something about you . . . I just like being with you. I mean, the sex was great—"

"It was."

"—but I liked the talking afterward just as much. And that's, like, not very common with me."

"Why is that?"

"Because most men start to snore about ten seconds after they come. So it kind of cuts the conversations down a little."

"Men your age," he said.

"Well, yeah."

"I normally don't have time for romantic assignations," he admitted. "So to meet someone I wish to see again is a rare and wonderful thing."

"What's an assignation? Because it sounds scarily like assassination."

"Tryst. Rendezvous."

"Oh. Well, that's okay. Maybe we should make a rule. We can talk about work but not about Caitlyn."

"As you wish."

"Although I will give you one piece of advice. Try backing off her. It works a lot better than the muscle, believe me."

"All right."

"And trust her. She's really smart. She was the smartest person I ever met, before I met you."

"Oh? I don't know whether to be flattered or horrified."

"Be flattered. But not too flattered. Don't, like, let it go to your head or anything."

"No, I won't do that." Pause. "She's always done well with conventional testing."

"Oh, yeah. Straight A's in school, without hardly trying. *So* annoying. And she reads, like, all the time. And she's, what d'you call it . . . eclectic! One time she came back from the library—it was so weird, I'll never forget it—anyway, she had a true crime book, the latest Harry Potter book, something by Shakespeare, and *Vogue*."

"That's eclectic all right."

"Yeah, anyway. Enough about her. We promised not to talk about her, right? Right. So, you're just picking at that. I've got nachos and a bottle of twenty-year-old Scotch back at my place. Let's book."

The Boss laughed and tossed his napkin on the table. "Madam, I am at your disposal."

Chapter 22

"So, your mom seems nice."

Dmitri looked up from the computer monitor. One of six, she noticed, on his desk, which was made of mahogany and a mere seven feet wide. Damn thing looked more like a moat than a piece of office furniture. "Oh, you're done for the day? Very well. I'll show you to your quarters."

"I'd rather have a tour of the Novakov family compound."

"You would? All right. Come along, then." He clicked a few keys, got up, and walked over to her. Once again, she was forced to control her drooling. God, had she ever seen a better-looking guy? And he even smelled great, he was wearing some sort of Stud-of-the-Month aftershave, something that smelled like cloves. Mmm . . . cloves . . .

". . . your session?"

"What?"

"I said, did you enjoy your session?"

"Oh, sure. Your mom's an okay lady. I mean, as okay as a prying head-peeper can be."

"Thank you," he said dryly.

"I can't believe I didn't figure it out before she told me. You guys look a lot alike. Same coloring."

"Yes, I have the Dauksa looks. The Novakovs tend to be short and blond."

Caitlyn thanked God for the Dauksas, whoever they were. "Yeah, I look like my mom too."

"Did she have the same eyes? I must confess," he confessed, leading her down a hallway, "I've never seen eyes that color before."

"Oh, chlorine-pool-colored?"

"Ah . . . yes, I suppose so. I was thinking more like the sky on the first day of spring."

"Nope. Chlorine pool. So, listen, she told me how you got the 'bytes. The bomb and all."

Dmitri's face was expressionless as he replied, "All right."

"That was probably a pretty bad scene. I just got cracked up in a limo accident."

"Quite a bad one, I understand."

"Yeah, it would have squished me good, normally," she said cheerfully. "By the way, you speak English great. I mean, I thought it was a little clipped, kind of British but not quite, but I couldn't quite put my finger on your accent. Not that you have much of one."

He didn't say anything.

"Hello? The nanobytes in your ears take the day off, or what?"

He smiled at her. She nearly gasped. Had she thought he'd been great-looking *before? Oh, Christ. I am in huge trouble.* "You didn't ask me a question," he explained, "so I didn't respond."

"Well, excuuuuuuuse me. So, you speak, like, a

bunch of languages? Did you know how to do that before the O.S.F. jammed all those nanos in your system?"

He paused, held open a door for her, then carefully replied, "I could speak English and Japanese before the . . . accident. Afterward, I could pick up languages much quicker."

"Because you don't forget anything."

"Yes."

"You got a chip in your head too? Mine talks to me. Bosses me around mostly. Drives me nuts. It's like having a voice in your head . . . one that's always right."

He burst out laughing, and she whimpered.

He had dimples.

"I am glad you decided to come back with me," he said when he finished his yuk-fest.

"Yeah, well. There wasn't anything good on TV tonight anyway."

Dmitri's admiration for Caitlyn James was growing by the moment. Her spur-of-the-moment decision to join him was looking less and less spur and more genius. Not that he'd ever had any doubts about her intelligence, because the O.S.F. did not hire idiots. But this!

He had the transcript of the session between her and his mother, and Caitlyn had done a pretty fair debriefing . . . a good trick, considering *she* had been the subject, not his mother. Now she was getting a good look at his home, and if she still meant to serve him to Gregory Hamlin on a plate, she was getting plenty of information on how to make that come about.

But through it all, she remained brightly cheerful, charming, and inquisitive, asking questions and often answering them herself. She was even able to talk about the bomb without him tightening up. He knew it was stupid and, worse, illogical, but he didn't like to talk about what had happened. With anyone. But somehow, with Caitlyn, it wasn't so bad.

You would have thought she was exactly as she seemed: a young woman without a care in the world, enjoying her first trip to Europe. Instead of what she was: a highly trained government assassin capable of breaking bones and smashing skulls to get what she needed.

"Why do you have black streaks in your hair?" he asked because he couldn't resist. Her hair was glorious, white blond and thick and almost perfectly straight, falling like a curtain to her shoulder blades. After he had knocked her out in the motel room, it had taken much of his self-control not to plunge his hands into it. "It would be so pretty if you were to let it be."

"Oh, it was a very serious day," she told him. "I had to go kick the jerk's ass first thing this morning. That called for black. You might have liked it better yesterday. Red highlights."

"Oh," he said, because it was, swear to God, all he could think of. Women—and there had been damned few of them since the accident—had always been a mystery to him. Then, "Here is my workout facility."

"Whoa," she responded, walking ahead of him as he held the door for her.

He tried to see the room—large as a gymnasium—through her eyes. Several dozen free weights,

several machines, and three high-powered treadmills, a German brand that wouldn't burn out until
he'd used them for at least eight months. The pool.
The ropes.

"You can work out?" she asked. "I mean, I knew
you didn't get that body eating Ho Ho's and drinking Kool-Aid and—"

"What is a Ho Ho?"

"Heaven on earth is what that is. But anyway, how
can you use these machines? Don't they break?"

"They are specially designed for me," he explained. "It takes much longer to wear them out. If
you're having trouble, you might try swimming
laps. You can go as quickly as you like and you certainly won't hurt a pool."

"Huh. Cool. I never thought of that." She ran her
hand over one of the free weights—fifty pounds—
absently lifted it out of the way with one hand, then
said, "I haven't been able to *really* work out for a
while. I shudder to imagine the cellulite encroach-
ing on my thighs."

He willed himself not to look at her legs, which
was difficult, as her black leggings left little to the
imagination. "You seem fine to me."

She grinned at him and patted the treadmill.
"Shall we see?"

Chapter 23

"Okay, okay, I give up! Enough!" Caitlyn allowed the treadmill to spit her onto the floor like an olive pit, and she collapsed to the gym mats. "Cripes! You're a machine! Uh, no offense."

Dmitri smirked down at her from his own treadmill. Damn. There was that dimple again, flickering at her from his left cheek . . . and gone just as quickly. "Do you need some water? Possibly a transfusion?"

"Ha fucking ha. No need to be such a smug bastard about it."

"Ah, but several people would tell you I *am* a smug bastard." He hit the button to slow the machine down, and the speed dropped from one hundred kilometers to eighty. His face was lightly sheened with sweat, but the crumb wasn't even out of breath. "I do apologize. I admit, I was curious . . . you're the, uh, what's the phrase? Newer model? I had doubts about my ability to keep up with you, frankly."

She shook her head. "Well, lay them to rest, big guy. I can hit your speed, but I can't keep it up as long as you can. Here I thought I was the only one in the world who could run as fast as a Ford Mustang."

"Sorry," he said smugly.

"Yeah, well, how are you behind the shampoo chair? Probably not too great. Yeah! It's rinse, *then* repeat, by the way."

He slowed to sixty kilometers. "You did quite well. You looked . . . impressive."

"Flattery will get you everywhere. After I pass out on this floor for a few hours, I'll make you buy me supper. You know," she said boldly, "we'd make a helluva team."

He looked straight at her. "I've had thoughts," he said without a trace of a dimple, "in that direction myself."

"Oooh, how . . . weird and unsettling. But in a nice way," she added hastily. "So. When's dinner in this joint?"

Chapter 24

"Mother, I just want to know one thing. Is she the killer?"

"I can't tell you that, son. Not without more sessions. And possibly not even then, unless she obligingly kills someone in front of me. That would help us narrow it down," Elena Balta added thoughtfully.

They were in the library, drinking cognac by the fireplace. They spoke in their mother tongue, Lithuanian, a rich and comforting sound to Dmitri's ears. And, more important, if the lovely Caitlyn were eavesdropping—if she were anything like him she could overhear a conversation from a floor away—she wouldn't know what they were saying. Nothing in her file suggested she could speak Lithuanian.

"When I'm with her, it's difficult to imagine her capable of cold-blooded murder, no matter what the provocation," he said. "But when I read the file . . . when I consider the facts . . . she's the prime suspect."

"But that would be in keeping with sociopathy," his mother pointed out. "They can be tremendously charismatic individuals. I admit I felt the force of her personality during our session. And while we're talking . . . I didn't have the chance to discuss this with you earlier—"

Uh-oh. "Yes?"

"Son, what is she doing here? What were you thinking? I can't even remember the last time you brought a woman here."

"*You* can't remember?"

"Hush. You left to put a stop to the murders, to clear your own name—it's no surprise the O.S.F. suspects you. But then you returned with . . . with . . ."

"She wanted to come," he said defensively. He got out of his chair and started running his hands over the collection of first editions on the east wall. "And I admit to curiosity. I've never met anyone else in my . . . my situation before. I was curious about other attributes she might have, ways she might be different from me in addition to the same. I—"

"Son. I spent three hours with her. Her attributes are obvious. I just hope you know what you're doing."

He turned to look at her, this woman, his mother, a woman gifted with a fine and crafty intelligence, a woman who nearly killed herself putting herself through medical school after the death of his father, a woman determined to give them both a good life. "I just wish I knew about her and the Wagner team. I was hoping you could find out."

"Well, my crystal ball is broken, but another one has been posted. Meantime, all I can do is work with her, and hopefully, we'll find things out."

"Hmph."

"For what it's worth, when I'm with the woman, when I'm talking to her and listening to her chatter on about various amusing things, I have trouble imagining her capable of such violence. But," she added, finishing her cognac in one gulp, "it would not be the first time a sociopath was able to fool a member of the psychiatric profession. By the way, who won?"

"Who won what?"

"The race. It's all over the castle that you two were working out together today."

"As a matter of fact, I did."

"Oh." His mother grinned at him. "Too bad. I love you more than my life, Deemie, but you can be unbearably arrogant at times. I was hoping this Caitlyn James would put you in your place. Heaven knows you need it."

"Thank you," he said dryly.

Chapter 25

She was getting ready for bed at the end of a very long, very strange day, when she heard a discreet tap at her chamber. Chamber, not room. A room was what she had back home, about thirteen by fifteen feet. These . . . quarters, whatever you'd call them—well, let's just say the attached bathroom was as big as her bedroom at home.

"Just a second," she said, and shrugged into the robe thoughtfully provided. In fact, that made her a little hot under the collar. Did Yummy Dmitri have so many lady friends that he kept whole closets full of women's clothes? Creepy. And annoying. And creepy. "Come in!"

Speak of the devil, there he was. He had changed clothes, was casually dressed in khaki shorts and a dark blue T-shirt. Since it was about ten below outside, that was admirable. Or stupid. "Good evening. I trust you've found everything you need?"

"Yes." *Ya big pig!* "What's up?"

"Oh, I was just . . . just passing by your room and I thought I'd . . . I'd check in on you."

"Okay, thanks. Listen, there's no central heating in this place, is there? Because I'm freezing my ass off."

"Oh, it's cold?" he said vaguely. "I hadn't noticed. I do apologize. I'll have someone come in and lay a fire for you," he added, nodding to the fireplace in the corner, a massive thing of marble and stone that looked big enough to roast an entire cow in.

"Swell."

There was a short silence, broken by his "I just finished talking with my mother."

"Okay."

"She thought you were . . . very charming."

"Good to know." What was with this guy? He was pretty much loitering in her room. Well, his room. It *was* his castle after all. It was almost like he had something on his mind but wasn't sure how to go about doing it. And though she'd known the Wolf less than twenty-four hours, she knew without a doubt that if something was on his mind, you knew about it. "So, well, what's the plan for tomorrow?"

"My mother would like to meet with you again. Nine o'clock, if it's not too much trouble."

"Uh-huh. I'll bet she does." Caitlyn grinned. "She's still trying to figure out if I'm a nut-job, right?"

"Right."

"Well, okay. And maybe we can work out together again. That was fun, earlier. I'd like to try the pool. That was a good idea, the pool."

"Yes. I agree. I—I enjoyed it immensely."

"Well, me too. I miss working out with someone. So, if we use the pool, is there a swimsuit I can borrow?"

"Y—"

"Ah-ha! Why? Why are there women's clothes all over the place?"

"Not all over the place," Dmitri replied, puzzled. "Just in your quarters. When you agreed to come home with me, I radioed ahead and had my staff pick up some clothes for you. Why? Don't you like them?"

"Oh. Oh! Yeah, they're fab. Thanks. Really. That was super thoughtful." Sweet and charming and soooo thoughtful! Oh, he was swell. "So, anyway, I was saying about working out, there's my friend Stacy, but she doesn't exactly work out with me. She doesn't even get sweaty. Just watches me and we talk and stuff."

"That's nice," he said absently, crossing the room to her. "There is something else I've been thinking about. Something else I think I would enjoy immensely."

Then he pulled her to him and kissed her. But "he kissed her" was a little like saying "he dropped the bomb and it went off." It felt like more, much more. His arms were around her with possessive, almost bruising strength, his mouth was on hers, his tongue parting her lips (which, to be fair, were open in surprise, so it wasn't exactly difficult), and he was pulling her against him so she was standing on tiptoe. And kissing him back, of course. Why not? It was the chance of a lifetime.

She brought her hands up and put them on his broad chest, warm even through his T-shirt. Her tongue touched his and she bit his lower lip lightly, and he made a sound, some sound, and tightened his grip.

"Well?" she gasped, pulling back. "Were you right? Did you enjoy it immensely?"

"I did, my *aušra*."

"What?"

"It means sunrise."

"Oh." His hands were at the belt of her robe, and she thought, *Bad, bad idea*, but her hands wouldn't move to stop him, just clutched his shoulders with desperate strength, strength that would probably hurt anyone else on the planet, strength he didn't notice as he spread her robe open and sucked in his breath.

"You surprised me with your knock," she teased. "I didn't have time to get a nightgown on."

"Thank God," he said, and pulled her down on the bed with him. His mouth was on her neck, pressing kisses to her throat, and she touched his black hair, which was as crisp-silky as she had imagined it would be. And his mouth! Oh, Christ, his mouth. Hot and skilled and hungry all at once, and she didn't care where he kissed her as long as he didn't stop. He had worked down to her shoulders, nibbled her collarbone, and his hand came up and closed over a breast, then began rubbing in slow, lazy circles, and she groaned as she felt her nipple harden against his palm.

"You are a banquet," he whispered, nuzzling her cleavage.

"You are . . . are . . ." Nope. No good. Words were not enough. You are too sublime? Too fabulous? Too amazing to be real? That last one was about right. "Uh . . ."

"Never mind," he said, and laughed, and sucked one of her nipples into his mouth.

Too good? Too damned skilled? Too inhuman? Did nanobytes make you a better lover? She'd ask a member of the Wagner team, except most of them were dead. Most of them—

She still felt like ripping his shirt and shorts off and riding him into the sunset, like Silver the horse, but now the cold hand of reason had her and she thought, *Am I really going to do it with a guy I think might be a killer?*

No.

Oh, God, she nearly wept. *Really? No? Stupid conscience!*

But it was no good. The file of the murdered men and woman flashed before her, Egghead #1 prominently among them. She hadn't liked him much, hadn't liked any of the doctors and lab guys much, but she hadn't killed them, and whoever had needed to be stopped and, even better, brought to justice.

Dmitri was licking her nipples with the keen concentration of a cat involved with cream, and judging by the hot, long lump throbbing against her thigh, enjoying himself as much as she was.

Too bad. She hadn't come here to get laid. Okay, that wasn't exactly true. But she'd *also* come here to find things out. And not how long Dmitri's dick was either, or what he could do with it, what he would do to *her* with it—

(Oh, God!)

—but what had happened to the Wagner team, and if the Wolf was responsible.

She put her hands on his shoulders and pushed. He didn't move. She thought, *Help me out, nanobytes, I need to get this guy off me*, and pushed again, and he went flying back and hit the floor with a sickening thump.

"What the *hell*?" he said, almost shouted, leaping to his feet. His face was flushed, and as she watched him visibly struggle to get himself under control, she thought nervously that he looked very, very dangerous . . . and capable of anything.

"Sorry," she said, trying not to pant. "But it's a bad idea."

"The *hell*," he said again, scowling at her.

Her fingers itched to be in his hair again, so she sat on her hands. Then remembered her robe was gaping open, and tied it closed. "I'm not here for that," she said. "And it better not be why you brought me here."

"It—it wasn't. But—but—"

Wow. The Wolf was practically stammering. She hardened her heart. "Like I said. Bad idea. Good night."

For a long moment he stared at her, and she wondered what she'd do if he didn't leave. *Fight him, I guess. Fight and probably lose, but I'd try. I'd try and he'd . . . he'd . . . what in the world would he do?*

She nearly cried as he glared at her. She had such a crush, and wanted him to think only nice things about her. She seriously doubted he was thinking anything nice right now. And it hadn't exactly been easy to push him away. *She* had needs too.

He muttered something in a language she assumed was Lithuanian, probably "cock tease," then stalked out and slammed the big old heavy door behind him.

She collapsed back on the bed and put her hands over her face. *Oh I am in so much trouble, because I want him like I want food and water, want him and need him, but I can't, we can't, because I don't know . . . don't know if he killed those people . . . and what's worse is, right now I don't especially care.*

She cried herself to sleep.

Dmitri listened to her crying, went to his bedroom door for the sixth time in three minutes, then let his hand drop before it could even twist the knob. She had chosen this, she had driven him away, and if she was regretting any actions, it was none of his and all of hers.

His pride hurt almost as much as . . . other things. Clearly, she wanted nothing to do with him, and he knew exactly why. He wasn't a whole man—without the nanobytes in his system, he would have been long dead. She knew it—hadn't she asked his mother about the accident? Hadn't she asked him about it—knew it and didn't want him, and who could blame her?

He could.

He should have known. She was so pretty and vivacious and smart and beautiful and charming and lovely, what did she want with someone like him? A cold man, a man many assumed had no heart . . . just a bunch of circuitry. He had been insane to even go to her room, a fact he had known *before* he'd gone. But the rule of his head wasn't enough, and finally he had gone.

And he had thought . . . had been so happy when she seemed to welcome his embrace, glory in his touch, and he'd never wanted any woman the way he had wanted her at that moment.

And then she had pushed him off her and sent him away.

He rested his forehead on his arms and closed his eyes.

Chapter 26

"Wake up. Caitlyn. Get up."

Time for school already? Well, she'd have Stacy go to class and take notes for her . . . no, not Stacy, she was probably still at last night's party . . . Deb? Jan? George?

"Caitlyn. Get up."

She rolled away from the command, but the hand shaking her shoulder would not be dislodged. "Oh, fuck," she said, opening her eyes. "Someone better be on fire."

Dmitri was there, had his hand on her, was shaking her awake. Dark stubble bloomed along his jaw, and she was staring so hard, she almost missed what he said. "There's been another murder."

"What?" She sat up so quickly, she got dizzy for a second. She glanced over at the window, but it was still dark. Her internal clock informed her it was 4:33 A.M. local time. "Where?"

"In the States, of course," he said impatiently. "The next-to-last member of the Wagner team is dead. The—Gregory Hamlin called. He asked us both to come."

She'd fallen asleep barely an hour before and it was hard to focus. Dmitri was dressed in the same shorts and shirt, and in a flash of insight she knew he hadn't slept, hadn't even been to bed. "Another . . . last night?"

"The body was found thirty minutes ago, this time in the O.S.F. lab. The killer is getting bolder."

"Or more desperate. Shit. Shit! Okay, give me a minute."

"You have ten. Then we're flying back to the States."

"We are, huh? Didn't know you missed the gang at O.S.F. so much."

He leveled her with a look. "People are dying."

"Yeah, thanks, I got the news flash. At least I know you're not the killer. And now you know I'm not the killer."

He blinked. "Yes. Quite right."

"Well, good. It was weird, staying in your castle and wondering if you were a slobbering psychopath. I'm sorry about last night," she added, because his jaw was clenched so hard, she expected to see him spit teeth out in another minute. "It's not that I didn't want to. It's just . . ."

"I understand," he said flatly. "Get dressed." And he was gone.

She groaned and climbed out of bed. Great way to start the morning. Pissed-off rogue agents and dead people. Fuck a duck.

"So, the Boss is expecting us?"

Silence. This was a big improvement over the

last hour of the flight, which had been filled with silence. He was pissed at her, and she couldn't blame him, but she also couldn't help a flash of irritation. Men were such babies when you told them No Way. Held it against you for days.

"Well, that's good," she said, pretending he had answered. "Because I'd hate to surprise that son of a bitch. He's bad enough when he's expecting me."

Silence, except for the occasional click as the Wolf typed a new command into his laptop.

"You know, this whole thing is just chock full of irony. Here we are, winging our way to the Boss to help him out, when I swore not only would I not work for him, but I wouldn't cross the street to spit on him if his ass was on fire."

Silence.

"Well, I'm glad we got all this straightened out," she said sarcastically. Abruptly, she stood. "I'm gonna check out your little pad on wings, if you don't mind. And even if you do."

She flounced toward the back of the plane. Though the jet could easily seat fifty people, only she, Dmitri, the pilot, the copilot, and an attendant were on board. The attendant, a petite redhead with Orphan Annie hair and the greenest eyes Caitlyn had ever seen was in the front, chatting with the copilot. Caitlyn had refused breakfast and an early morning cocktail, being too wired and weirded out to eat or drink. Maybe later.

She tapped on a small door she assumed was a bathroom and, when nobody told her to fuck off, pushed it open.

It wasn't a bathroom. It was the tiniest, most perfect-looking bedroom she'd ever seen. There was a twin bed, made up with military precision—

if she sat on it, she'd bounce—and loads of pillows. There were three tiny windows so she could see out, and a small desk and chair. There was even a miniature refrigerator in the corner, which brought her back to her and Stacy's dorm days. Their little fridge had always been full of Zima and cottage cheese and chocolate milk. The combination wasn't so bad once you had enough Zimas in you.

She turned to go—and smacked right into Dmitri's chest. That was weird, if slightly yummy. He'd obviously followed her to the back of the jet, which was way better than ignoring her.

"What—" was all she got out before he kicked the door shut behind him and thumbed the lock. "Oh."

Still, he didn't say a word, just looked at her with his intense gaze, and she had the oddest feeling . . . almost like he was hurt, like she had harmed him. Ha! Like a mirage could ever hurt a wolf.

He pushed her back toward the bed and she went, willingly enough. There wasn't any reason to send him away now . . . he wasn't the killer. And she still wanted him from last night. Shit, wanted him from seeing him at her party, would want him anytime, anywhere.

But as he pulled her shirt over her head, as he rapidly disrobed, as her leggings went flying, she had to wonder: Did she want this right now, this way? It was almost like he was . . . punishing her.

She decided, when his tongue thrust past her teeth, when he plunged his hands into her hair and pressed her to him, that she did. If he was mad and wanted to pay her back, fine. She'd worry about what it all meant . . . later. She'd worry later.

Right now the lust that had kept her awake, the

desire that had made her cry herself to sleep, had flared back to life, had come surging back the moment she heard the lock click home. Stupid to play Outraged Virgin right now . . . not when they both needed exactly the same thing.

He lifted her to him and she felt her back against the wall—literally!—and then he was parting her with rough fingers and surging inside her. It hurt, but oh, it was good at the same time, it was what she'd needed. She wrapped her legs around his waist and he held her easily, and pumped, pumped, pumped.

She groaned and he said through gritted teeth, "Hurts?"

"Yes."

"Shall I stop?"

"No," she said, and when she heard her voice she was surprised—was that sweetly husky tone hers? It seemed to affect him too, because he closed his eyes and shuddered. And all the while he was pumping against her and holding her, his hands easily supporting her in the air, clutching the backs of her thighs.

His very roughness, his absorption, the fact that she was pinned to the wall like a butterfly to the board, pinned by a cock that was digging into her, making her his, all that was enough to jolt her into orgasm.

He shuddered again, and for a moment his grip tightened to the point of pain, and then he was setting her on the floor, sliding out of her. She tried to stand but her knees buckled, and he caught her and swung her onto the bed.

"What was *that*?" she gasped.

He didn't say anything, just got dressed and readjusted his clothing. After a long, difficult moment he said, "I apologize."

"Don't be a jackass."

"I—have no excuse. Don't . . . don't be afraid." His gaze was haggard, haunted. "Everyone is afraid of me."

She rolled her eyes. "I'm *not* afraid, idiot. But I am hungry. You think the flight attendant can rustle up some scrambled eggs?"

He looked at her, visibly surprised, then turned and left the room.

The eggs were waiting for her by the time she got dressed.

Chapter 27

"**D**mitri Novakov! What an unexpected pleasure." The Boss looked them both over, then chuckled. "An embarrassment of riches, to be sure."

"You suck," Caitlyn informed him, bringing a ghost of a smile to Dmitri's face, a smile that disappeared as suddenly as it had shown up. "In every possible way. Now you've got lab weenies being axed in your own offices? How lame is that? How lame are *you*? This place is lousy with security."

"Not lousy enough, apparently. Thank you both for coming, and so quickly too. Have a seat," he added, gesturing to the two chairs in front of his desk.

"Pass. Getting all comfy and chatty in here is nowhere on my to-do list. So, what? Everyone on the Wagner team is dead now?"

"Almost. There's one left, Dr. Roe. She's in protective custody this minute."

"Well, finally. It took only . . . what? Four murders?"

The Boss didn't say anything, but looked stricken for a moment, such a brief moment quickly followed by his usual blank-faced imperturbability that she wondered if she'd imagined the expression.

"Well, great," Caitlyn fretted, resisting the impulse to pace. "This is all just . . . great."

"You're so quiet, Dmitri," the Boss said, glancing over at him. It was impossible to tell how the odious, evil man felt about the Wolf being there. "How uncharacteristic."

"His skin's crawling just being on the same city block as you, creep, and I know exactly how he feels."

"Right," Dmitri said, that small smile back. She was so glad to see it. He'd been odd after their mutual introduction into the Mile-High Club. Even quieter and more withdrawn than earlier, if that was possible.

"He thinks you're the evilest man in the universe," she continued, "just like I do, and for two cents he'd let you solve your own problems and fuck Dr. Roe."

"Right," Dmitri said, his smile broadening.

"Fuck poor defenseless Dr. Roe?" the Boss mock-gasped.

"Fuck you too," Caitlyn replied rudely.

"Caitlyn, Caitlyn. Really, it pains me that we're at odds all the time. Actually, I've come to realize of late that you and I have much more in common than I ever imagined."

She made throwing-up noises and Dmitri tightened his lips, looking like someone struggling with laughter. Well, maybe he had a bellyache. "We don't have anything in common, you ogre."

The Boss sniffed. "Ah, the soul of maturity, even in a crisis."

"Blow me," she said. "So, what? What now? You want us to do our bloodhound routine, talk to the cops, what?"

"We have not involved the police. And I haven't allowed anyone in the lab. The crime scene is exactly the way it was when the killer left."

"Oh, gross," she said, knowing where this was going.

"Why don't you two go check it out? Then report back here."

"We'll check it out," Dmitri said quietly, "but we won't be reporting to you."

"Fine, fine, have it your way. Oh, and, Caitlyn?"

"What?"

"Stacy says hi."

Caitlyn blinked and stopped halfway to the door, so suddenly that Dmitri bumped into her, but she was so surprised by what the jerk had said, she barely felt the shock of his body against hers. She slowly turned, gently shoved Dmitri out of her sight line, and said, "What? What did you say?"

The jerk raised his pale eyebrows and feigned surprise at her surprise. "Stacy. Your best friend? Lovely girl, medium height, skin the color of cappuccino, limbs like silk? Is any of this ringing a bell, dear?"

"What?"

"When I left her last night—this morning, actually, after security called—she asked me to say hello when I saw you. Also, 'Tell that girl she's almost out of margarita mix.' "

Caitlyn digested this for a moment, then said, almost pleaded, "You're not fucking my friend."

"Actually, I really am. She—*gak!*" Caitlyn had crossed the room and was holding him off the floor, shaking him like a rag. "Let go! Stacy loves this suit!"

"Die," she said through gritted teeth, tightening her grip. The pervert turned a dark shade of plum and gargled something she couldn't understand. "Die! Right now."

"Now, Caitlyn," Dmitri said, the first time he'd said anything directly to her besides "Buckle your seat belt" when they were about to land. "I agree, if anyone deserves death by strangulation, it's him. In fact, under most circumstances, I would gladly lend you a hand. Two, if you needed them. But do you think it's wise? At this particular moment in time? There will be plenty of opportunities to take care of this. Later."

The swine gargled something in agreement.

"Won't take a minute," she snarled. "Then we can go check out the lab. Then I can puke. Then I can cry myself to sleep again. Then I can tell Stacy it's time to find a new fuck buddy."

Dmitri shrugged. "Oh, have it your way." He smiled at the Boss. "Sorry."

"Girlfriend, you put him down *right now*."

They both turned. Stacy was standing in the doorway, bizarrely arrayed in a typical outfit: forest green leggings, a sky blue T-shirt, a black leather jacket that was two sizes too big for her, red tennis shoes. Her hair was pulled back so far, her black eyebrows looked like they were arched in surprise, and she was holding a Brueger's Bagels bag.

Caitlyn put him down. Sort of.

"That must have been six feet," Dmitri said, watching the creep soar through the air and crash against the far wall. "Oh, well done."

"I came to bring you some breakfast, seemed like you'd be having a long day," Stacy explained, staring at the crumpled lump. "Good thing I stopped by. And it was super sweet of you to tell your secretary to let me in whenever I came to visit, BTW."

"Anytime, my darling," the Boss groaned from the floor.

Caitlyn shuddered. "Stacy, say it ain't so! He was just torturing me for fun, right? It's not true, right? Right? *Right?*"

"Jimmy, I love you, but if you ever do that again, I'll snatch you bald-headed."

Caitlyn clutched a hank of her hair protectively. "You wouldn't!"

"Oh yes I would." Giving her a good glare, Stacy pushed past them and bent over the lump on the floor that was the Boss. "Greg, you okay?"

"I am now . . . darling."

Caitlyn snarled and took a step forward, but Dmitri's hand closed over her arm and he pulled her back. "Death is too good for you! I'll pull your skin off in strips! I'll tie you to the back bumper of my car and drag you down Lake Street. I'll—"

"Jimmy, *enough.*" Stacy helped the cretin to his feet and shook her head. "Cripes. I knew you wouldn't exactly be thrilled by the news, but I didn't think it'd be this bad."

"Thrilled? *Thrilled?* Have you *lost your fucking mind?* This guy . . . *this* guy! You *know* what he's like. I told you all the things—"

"He saved you," she said quietly. "I'd have liked him for that, if for no other reason, you know?"

"Yeah, saved me for what?" Caitlyn asked bitterly.

"And we're not doing it just for fun, though it started out that way. I really like him. He's—he's not like anybody in the world."

"Thank you, darling."

"*You shut up*. Started out that way? How long has this been going on? Cripes, how long was I in Europe?" Caitlyn looked around wildly for a clock. "What year is it?"

"It's been a whirlwind courtship," the Boss croaked modestly, rubbing his throat, where an interesting bruise was already forming.

"*Stop talking*. Stacy, wh-why him? Of all the guys in the world, why *that* guy?"

"I don't know, Jimmy. I really don't. And if you ever told me I'd—there's just something about him. I can't explain it, and now's not the time even if I could," Stacy said, glancing over at Dmitri.

"Oh, don't mind me," he said, struggling against laughter.

Stacy looked back at Caitlyn. "And I don't know where this is going or even if it will last, but I do know this: you try to hurt him again and I'll make you sorry. I don't care if you *can* lift a Porsche over your head. I'll figure out a way to make you sorry."

Caitlyn clutched her head. "This can't be happening. It's all some totally fucked-up dream."

"At the very least," Dmitri commented, "it's been worth the trip."

"Uck. Let's go. I'll talk to *you* later," she said to Stacy, who, to her credit, shrugged and didn't look remotely alarmed. "You I'm never, ever speaking to again," she told the Boss.

"Don't tease, dear," he said as she stomped out the door.

Chapter 28

"I'm gonna barf! I mean right now! Ride the vomit comet, toss my cookies, shout at the floor—pick your saying."

"It certainly seemed like a surprise," Dmitri commented, his hands in his pockets as they followed the security guard to the lab. "Lord knows *you* were surprised."

"A surprise? No, Dmitri. A surprise is when someone hands you a present and it's not your birthday. A surprise is when a pal picks up the drink tab when you were supposed to go dutch. This is a total fucking shock, representing the beginning of the end of human society."

Dmitri snorted.

"Yuk it up, pal. Meanwhile, my world is crumbling around me. Frankly, I was gonna bug you about what happened on the jet, but all I can think about right now is . . . is . . . how could she? Him I get, he'll do anything to torture me, but what was *she* thinking?"

"As much as it pains me to say anything remotely positive about Gregory Hamlin, I'm not sure his . . . assignations . . . with your friend are about you at all."

"What the hell are you talking about?"

"She knows his real name," he explained quietly. "It took me eight years to find out his real name. The only way your friend could know is if he told her. And he never tells anyone."

"So, what? What are you saying?"

"I'm merely suggesting there might be more to this than you think."

"Gawd. I don't know if that makes me feel better or worse." She paused for a moment. "Worse. A million times worse. Bad enough if they're doing it just for the hell of it. But if they're in a relationship . . ." Caitlyn shook her head. "Well, she's ruined Christmas, that's for sure."

"Your friend seems very . . . sure of herself."

"She's the stubbornest person in the world," Caitlyn snapped.

"And it was interesting, the way she defended him."

"Interesting like horrifying? Interesting like really, really weird and fucked-up? Interesting like being trapped in a waking nightmare? Help me out here."

"Just . . . interesting."

"This is it," the security guy (M. Daniels, his name tag read, and what kind of a name was M?) announced. "Room six twenty-four. Dr. Miller's still in there. If you could tell me when you're done, I'll get the room processed."

"Very good," Dmitri said.

The guard stood there while Dmitri opened the door (holding a handkerchief in his hand as he did so, Caitlyn noticed) and walked in. After a moment, she followed.

Chapter 29

She couldn't see the body at first. All the shades were drawn and the lab was on the south side of the building, so there was little natural light. But when she spotted it, she wondered how she had missed it. Dr. Miller was sprawled behind one of the lab counters, but his arm was sticking out and his fingernails were blue.

"Watch where you step," Dmitri said calmly, and walked around the body, studying it. "Hmm. Body temperature has dropped only ten degrees. He hasn't been dead long."

"Swell," she muttered. It occurred to her that she had never seen a dead body before except on television, and that it wasn't much fun. Not that she'd thought it would be a laugh a minute, but it was even less fun than she imagined.

It wasn't much like television. Dr. Miller didn't look like he was sleeping. He looked freaked out and deader than shit. His skin was waxy, almost yellowish, and she thought if she had to touch his dead hand or his dead face, she'd scream and scream and finally go crazy. The perfect end to a perfect day.

She noticed his lab coat had bloody holes in it and, after scanning, realized that there were two bullets in his left lung and one in his heart. But there wasn't much blood, certainly not as much as TV would have a viewer believe.

"Multiple gunshots to the chest," Dmitri said absently. "But who could get a gun into this place?"

"Only any agent."

"Right. But those guns will be on record, will be in a databank somewhere. We might ask Gregory Hamlin if any agents have reported missing weapons."

"Or," she said, "I could ask him to die slowly and in great pain."

"It's refreshing to find a kindred soul."

"Yeah, yeah."

"I admit, I found your treatment of him vastly amusing."

"So glad I could help. Let's stay focused so we can get the hell out of here, okay? Like this place doesn't bug me enough without dead bodies glaring up at me. Fuck a duck. So, what? The bad guy came in and shot Dr. Miller, then left? Got through security, brought a gun, then got back out through security? Come on."

"Well," Dmitri said, "think about what that means for a moment."

She thought. Then, "Oh."

"Right."

"Oh!"

"Right. And if you and I have thought of it, doubtless Gregory Hamlin has also thought of it."

"I hate having to clean his fucking house."

Dmitri shrugged. "It's the way of the world. I have to admit, the dreading of coming back to this place was far worse than actually being here."

"Oh." She thought that over. "Yeah, sorry about that. I guess I sort of forgot how hard this might be for you."

He grinned in the gloom of the lab. She was pissed as hell at the dork and Stacy, but not so pissed that the flash of that dimple didn't still weaken her knees. "You had other things to think about."

"Boy, that's the truth," she muttered.

Then, after a long moment, he said, "Cry yourself to sleep again?"

"What?"

"In the office. You said, 'Then we can go check out the lab, then I can puke, then I can cry myself to sleep again.' "

"Well, duh," she said irritably. She would never be able to follow the track of his mind. Shouldn't they be trying to solve a murder right now? Men! Or maybe it was cyborgs! "Think I wanted to send you away last night? It was the hardest thing I ever had to do. Even harder than passing Introduction to Physics. But I couldn't sleep with you, wondering if you were the killer. Duh."

He stared at her expressionlessly for a moment, then slowly smiled. It was like watching the sun come up, and she forgot her annoyance. "That's . . . that's why you sent me away?"

"Stop me if you've heard this before: duh! Why *else* would I send you away? Because I hate broad shoulders and six-pack abs? Because great kissing makes me ralph? Jesus Christ!"

"I thought . . . never mind what I thought." But

he looked quite cheerful, weirdly cheerful given where they were. "Ah . . . it's shaping up to be quite a nice day, don't you think?"

She stared at him. "Dude, you are *weird*."

Chapter 30

"I'd invite you to stay at my place—it's the least I can do, since you put me up at your castle and had your mom try to shrink my brain—but Stacy's staying with me right now and it'll be tight."

Dmitri almost shuddered. "That's quite all right. It's probably best you and Stacy have privacy while you . . . discuss things."

"I'd like to discuss things," Caitlyn muttered, stomping through the lobby of the Minneapolis Marriott. "Right upside her head, I'd like to discuss things."

"I prefer a well-run hotel to most homes anyway," he said.

"How annoyingly bacheloresque. So, what?" she asked, stepping into the plush elevator behind him. "They're processing poor deader-than-shit Dr. Miller, and now what?"

"Let me get my laptop set up, and I'll show you. For starters, we'll pull files on all O.S.F. employees, find out who, if anyone, is missing a gun, find out who has access to the Wagner team."

"You can do that? Just from your laptop?"

He smiled at her and said nothing.

"Can I do that, maybe? Someday?"

"Probably." He added, "I could teach you if you wish."

"Oh. Okay." She wasn't sure how she felt about that. Was it cool, or unbearably geeky? Well, she'd think about it later. "Maybe I'll take you up on that. Listen, I'll have the driver take me home and get my car. And change my clothes! Then I can come back and take you wherever you want. That way the O.S.F. doesn't necessarily know every move we make."

"I'm sure your car is bugged. But if it makes you feel better to drive your own car . . ." He shrugged.

"Oh, man. This day . . . it's just getting better and better. Should have stayed in bed."

"I'm wondering if it might not be Dr. Roe," Dmitri said thoughtfully, following her as she lunged out of the elevator.

"The last member of the team? How come?"

"Everyone else is dead."

"Yeah, but what's her motive?"

"It could be any of a number of things. Professional jealousy, for one."

"Yuck. Helluva dumb reason to plug someone. A whole bunch of someones."

"Someone like you wouldn't understand the darker regions of a person's heart."

"Okaaaaaaay." Whatever the hell that meant. She was so freaked out by the day's events that it was harder than usual to know what the hell Dmitri was babbling about. "I think it's the swine."

"Really? What's his motive?"

"Ha! He's so wicked and horrible, he doesn't need one. He probably kills employees for relaxation, you know, like most guys play racquetball."

"Dislike Gregory Hamlin as I do, I doubt he's the killer. He runs the department, they all do things on his orders. His annual budget is in the eight figures, and he has the ear of the president. The last thing he would do is start killing off the team that made us."

"Why? Because he wants to make more?"

Again, that maddening shrug.

"Well, fuck that! Jeez, the killer's actually doing us a favor."

"That's one way of looking at it," Dmitri said carefully, popping his key card into the suite's slot. "It's why you and I were suspects, remember."

"Huh." Then, "Whoa!" The suite was amazing . . . dark, rich carpeting, a piano (in a hotel room!), multiple rooms, and, when she darted into the bathroom, an enormous Jacuzzi tub in dark gray marble. "Holy cow! This isn't a hotel room, it's . . . er . . ." She couldn't think of anything fancy enough.

"Their Presidential Suite is quite nice," Dmitri remarked, already setting up his laptop.

"Nice? Kitties are nice. This place is like a fucking palace. And I would know!"

"Mmmm," he said, already absorbed. Then he looked up at her. "Another suspect . . . now, don't get angry. . . ."

"Dude, have you been paying attention lately at all?"

"Fair enough. I'm wondering if the killer might not be your friend."

"Stacy?" Caitlyn burst out laughing, finally collapsing on a chair opposite the desk. "Oh, man. Thanks. I really needed cheering up."

"She has cause to resent the Wagner team," he pointed out. "And now, thanks to her . . . ah . . . social connection, she can apparently enter this building anytime she wishes."

"Dmitri, you're so far out of left field, you're not even in the ballpark anymore. Stacy wouldn't hurt a fly. Literally. She shoos them out the window. Says it's bad karma to squash anything, even a bug."

He shrugged. "It's just another working theory."

"Well, think of a different one."

She prowled around the spacious suite for a few minutes, wondering exactly what happened next. She wasn't a homicide detective, she did heads. She had told the fink that she wasn't qualified for this job. Watching Dmitri peck away at a laptop that was probably worth ten grand, that fact was brought home to her all over again.

What made matters worse was, the fink wasn't even involving the police. He thought it was an inside job—and she had to agree—and he expected her and the Wolf to clean up the mess.

So now the Wolf was engrossed in work, the Boss was doing whatever it was he did (foreclose on orphanages? Tear down homeless shelters?), and she was . . . was . . . what?

Tired. Very, very tired. Her sleepless night was catching up with her, not to mention jet lag and the stressful events of the day. There was a perfectly nice bed somewhere in this suite, and she meant to find it and have a nap. Couldn't do anything while Dmitri was working anyway.

She found the bed after searching for a minute

and was asleep five seconds after her head hit the pillow.

"Caitlyn."

Great. It was Dmitri, waking her up to tell her there'd been another murder. They'd have to fly back to the States, like, immediately. He was pissed at her, too, not that she could blame him, and when they were on the jet, he'd—

Wait. That had already happened.

She opened her eyes to find him bending over her. This was startling, yet yummy. "Guess I fell asleep. What's up? Are you done?"

He shook his head, but his intense blue eyes never left her face. "I'm crunching data right now. Nothing to do but wait."

"Okay." She yawned. "So we wait."

"Yes. Forgive me, but I've been wanting to do this for hours."

"Wanting to . . . ? Mmmph." His mouth was on hers again, his fingers twined in her hair. She broke the kiss after a delightful long minute and gasped, "You—you want to? Again?"

"More than anything."

"But . . . I thought you didn't like me. You seemed really mad before. You seemed . . ."

"I was mad," he said soberly, playing with a hank of her hair. "I was . . . a fool. Of course I like you. I *adore* you."

"Dmitri . . . I'm not trying to rub anything in, but if you felt that way, why—"

He shook his head sorrowfully. "You're quite right. I shouldn't have taken you in the jet like a— but I was . . . I was angry. Upset about last night. As a matter of fact, if you send me away again, I don't think I'll survive it."

"No pressure though," she teased. "Lucky for you I'm on the Pill. And I didn't get a chance to ask you this earlier, but I assume the nanobytes keep you from being crawling with disease."

"Quite," he said dryly, then laughed as she tugged him toward her. Not by his hand. "Wait, I still have my shoes on. Not to mention everything else."

"Well, jeez, come *on*!" She was tempted to prolong the scene with pouting and listen to him beg for forgiveness, but frankly, she was too eager for sex to torture him. Maybe next time. "Come on, come on, come on!"

"All right, all right, don't tear my shirt off . . . well, all right, do that if you wish. I have lots of shirts."

"What a relief," she said, and pulled so hard, buttons went flying and skittering across the room. She heard the double thud as his shoes hit the floor, and then, oh glory be, his hands were on her, the hands she'd ached for all last night, the hands that were on her for all too brief a time in the jet. They were in her hair, they were running over her limbs, they were caressing her breasts, and she was kissing him and running her own hands across his broad, hard shoulders.

"Don't stop," she groaned as he licked the tender undersides of her breasts. "Oh, God, I don't want you to stop."

"Again, we are of like minds." His voice was muffled against her flesh. "Oh, Caitlyn. You are sublime."

She was sublime? Had he looked in a mirror? Ever? His strong hands were everywhere, his mouth was everywhere, the clothes were everywhere, and she didn't give a rat's ass.

Now he was moving lower and was kissing the light fuzz over her pubic bone, and now his tongue was opening her like a flower, stroking and licking the damp folds.

Oh, God, he was better than her vibrator, Big Blue! In her vast sexual experience (more than the late Mother Teresa, fewer than Stacy), most men would go there to get her wet so they could stop as soon as possible and get what they needed, but Dmitri showed no signs of leaving, almost like the act itself was pleasurable to him.

His tongue and lips were amazing, and when she felt his mouth settle over her throbbing clit at the exact moment a finger slipped up inside her, she nearly screamed at the bold sweetness of it.

He worked her to orgasm again and again using fingers and tongue, chuckled when she shuddered and clutched at his shoulders, laughed outright when she begged him to fuck her, to stop what he was doing down there and come up here and *fuck her now.*

Finally, oh, finally, he was licking her stomach and then her cleavage and then his broad chest was settling over hers and she wrapped her legs around his waist and whimpered into his neck when he parted her with trembling fingers and slowly slid inside her.

He was whispering into her hair as he eased into her, whispering in a language that sounded sweet and dark, and when he started to thrust, she thought she would die, die with a silly grin on her face, die happy, die well.

She rose to meet him, and their stomachs slapped together in a beat that was as old as the family of man. He was still whispering in that secret language, but now his tone was more urgent, his thrusts more demanding, and she met him with everything she had, met him and wordlessly demanded more.

"God," he said when she shuddered and clenched around him. "God, God . . . Caitlyn, my bold one, my own . . ."

"It's so good," she gasped, almost wept. "It feels so good."

Her words seemed to do something to him, push him over some edge that he couldn't come back from, and he stiffened in her arms and then shivered all over.

She could feel him pulsing within her and, for an odd moment, wished she weren't on the Pill, wished he were making her pregnant at that very moment, pregnant with his baby, a boy or girl with his hair and her eyes. A strange thought and one she had never had at such a moment, not with any man.

She wept, and she didn't know why, and he held her, and kissed her tears, and when she slipped back into sleep, he was whispering in that dark language again.

Chapter 31

"**Y**ou had sex! Again!" Stacy cried as soon as Caitlyn stepped through her front door.

"Cripes. What are you, a witch?" Caitlyn had been planning on giving Stacy the cold shoulder, being chilly and distant and standoffish and absolutely *no* margarita parties until her friend regained her senses, stopped taking drugs (was there any other explanation? Caitlyn thought not), and killed the Boss. Or dumped him. No, killed him.

But she had forgotten Stacy's uncanny instincts and had been startled into answering her. "You and I are not talking about my sex life until you fix yours. And I mean, like, yesterday."

Stacy hurried toward her from the couch and peered at her. "Wow, you *totally* did it! I mean, I knew this morning, but I was kind of distracted by trying to stop you from squishing my new guy like a bug."

"Don't remind me. And don't call him the new guy. Let's call him the dead guy."

She ignored that. "Greg said you were back in town to do some work for him—"

"I. Will. Kill! Him! How many times do I have to tell people, I don't work for him!" Her fingers plunged into her hair and she had to actively restrain herself from pulling hard. "Arrrrgggghhh!"

"—and here you've been bumping hips . . . you did it with that unbelievably delish-looking guy in the office, right? Right? Oh, man! That hair! Those eyes! Those *shoulders*."

"Well . . ."

"Oh my God, he is so gorgeous!" Stacy rhapsodized. "All tall and cool and yummy, and those big hands and those eyes . . ."

"All this is true," Caitlyn said modestly, calming down and pulling her hands out of her hair.

"So . . . ?"

She knew where this was going. She also knew Stacy would be merciless until she'd gotten all the answers. Quicker—and easier—to just come clean. "Best in my life."

And not just because of the sensations Dmitri had aroused in her. Not because she was so desperately, wildly attracted to him. The jet had been fine, but their time in the suite . . . it had been . . . more. The way he looked when she came, the way he whispered dark, delicious things into her ear, the way he held her after. For the first time, she truly understood the phrase "making love." It hadn't been fucking, that was for sure. "Very, super, amazing, ultrabest."

"I'll bet. He looks like he knows what he's doing."

You don't know the half of it. Force of habit—she'd been telling Stacy all her secrets for over five years—almost made her say, *Best of all, most wonder-*

ful of all, he's a cyborg like I am. The only other one in the world.

But no. Tempting as it was to unload on her friend, that was Dmitri's secret to tell. Not hers.

"Let's get off the subject of my sex life and get back to yours."

"Let's not. I had enough of that this morning. You're not going to throw me into a wall, are you? Because that looked, like, so massively painful."

"Good. I hope I cracked all his ribs. I hope bone shards are puncturing his lungs this minute. If he's sore or, even better, in the ICU, he won't be able to . . . um . . . I mean he won't . . . "

"Never underestimate the inventiveness of an older man," Stacy said solemnly, ignoring Caitlyn's all-over shudder.

She managed to get herself under control long enough to whine, "Why, Stace, why? That's the one thing I gotta know. Out of all the men. All the bad, sucky, disastrous choices you could make. After all the things I told you. Why *him*?"

"Come into the kitchen," Stacy said gently. "I've got coffee made."

When they were seated at the kitchen island, Caitlyn sulkily sipping coffee heavily laced with cream and sugar, and Stacy drinking nothing at all, she continued. "Honestly, Jimmy, I couldn't even tell you. How can I explain it to anyone, even my best friend, when I don't know myself? I was always grateful to those government weenies for saving you."

"But—"

"I know, I know. Don't you think I understand how you feel? I was there when Gregory sent those goons after you. I saw what had changed, how you were changed. I mean, cripes, in school you couldn't even do the five-hundred-yard dash without needing, like, transfusions afterward, but now all of a sudden you're like Supergirl. I know you like to go your own way and I know you don't like to be under obligation . . . to anyone. But still. I couldn't help it. . . . I was so glad you were alive."

Caitlyn took a moody slurp.

"So I always told myself if I ever ran into him, this guy who took over your life, the Boss, I'd thank him. Fat chance, right? How's someone like me ever going to meet someone like him? I didn't expect to see him at the party last week, to say the least! And I really didn't expect to find him . . . to think he was . . ." She shook her head. "I can't explain it. And it wasn't like it sometimes is, all heat and nothing else. We talk, you know, and discuss things, and have fun, and he has the greatest laugh and the sweetest smile. . . ."

He has a nasty chuckle, Caitlyn thought, *and he doesn't smile, he smirks*. But she didn't say anything. Her anger at her friend was rapidly fading, to be replaced by a kind of dull despair. Stacy was falling for the Boss. Soon the world would burst into flames and then things would really get sucky.

"And like I said, I don't know where it's going with him or even if it's going anywhere, but I'm kind of interested in sticking around for the ride, you know?"

"Umf," she replied. "Stace, um, I heard every word you said. . . ." And the chip in her head would probably play it back a thousand times, putting her in her own special hell. "But do you ever wonder what the j—what he wants out of all this? What he's up to? It can't be just, you know, getting laid. I mean, I know guys are nuts about you, so I figured ages ago you must be a great lay. . . ."

"Yeah, well," she said modestly.

"But don't you, um, think it's kind of weird that out of all the women in the world, he picked my best friend?"

Stacy's dark eyes met Caitlyn's without flinching. "It's not like that, Jimmy."

"Okay."

"I don't expect you to be happy about it, but I expect you not to break his neck or run him over or crack his spine or whatever you'd like to do in order to let off steam."

"Umf."

"What are you doing back here anyway? I thought you had a bunch of murders to solve. I mean, I was hanging around hoping you'd show, but I was still kind of surprised when you came in the door."

"Well, yeah, I do—I mean, Dmitri and I do. But what am I supposed to do, Stace? I'm in that lab, looking at the dead guy and trying not to puke, and I don't even know how to dust for fingerprints. Like I've been saying, I'm not a cop. This isn't my thing at all. We looked at dead Dr. Miller and putzed around the lab and then Dmitri started with his computer thing and then I had the best sex of my life and took a nap, and now I'm here to shower and change my clothes and get my own car. But as far as solving the murders, I dunno. I really don't."

"Fair enough. Like you said, it's not like you didn't warn everybody, right?"

"Right. And next time you're cuddling with the Boss, you might want to remind him."

"Nope. We promised each other not to talk about you when we're . . . you know. Together."

"You mean, the *one* thing that might make this horribly nasty situation work for me, and you won't do it?"

"Nope."

"Fuck a duck!"

"On your own time, sweetie. Now. Let's talk about Mr. Yummypants."

Caitlyn scowled, then said, "He's from Lithuania, he has his own castle, he's helping me on a case, he likes me, he's fabulous in bed, and I'm in deep, deep trouble."

"Oh, good," she sighed, pouring herself a cup of coffee. "Tell me all about it."

Chapter 32

"Well, you've fixed things fine, haven't you?" Caitlyn snapped, slamming the door so hard, it rattled in its frame.

The Boss didn't look up from his paperwork. "Fine, thanks, dear, and you?"

"Aw, shut the hell up. I don't know what you're up to with Stacy, but when you're done torturing me and you toss her aside like yesterday's meat loaf, your ass is *mine*. You can't even *imagine* the things I'll do to you. They'll write books about it."

At last he looked up. His hair was sleeker and darker than ever and his eyebrows just as weirdly pale. He still looked like an evil egg to her. What Stacy saw in him . . . she just couldn't imagine it.

"Caitlyn, it pains me on several levels to break this to you, but my relationship with Stacy has absolutely nothing to do with you. I realize that must come as a shock, so give yourself all the time you need to process the implications."

"Aw, shut the hell up. Where's Dmitri?"

The Boss shrugged. Oh, sure. Like he didn't know every movement the Wolf was making.

The Boss must have read her mind—like he didn't have enough bad habits—because he added, "I really don't. He can fool all our tracking devices. Believe me, I'd like to know. But he could be standing in the next room and I wouldn't know it . . . and neither would you."

Caitlyn opened her mouth, then shut it when she remembered that on her nanoscans, Dmitri showed up as a regular guy. When he most certainly was not.

"Run along," the Boss told her cheerfully.

"Listen. About Stacy. I'll tell you what. Break up with her and I'll stay here and work for you for . . . um . . . a year."

"Ten years."

"*Two* years."

"Five years."

"Fine, fine, five years. But you'll break up with her? Call her. Call her right now."

The Boss looked at her for a long moment, then said, smiling, "No."

"What?"

"N-o. As in, I decline. As in, I'd rather have Stacy in my life and you out of it."

"But . . . but you want me to work for you! It's what you've been after since day one!"

"Yes, but not that badly. Not badly enough to hurt Stacy."

"But it's for the good of the country!"

The Boss shrugged.

Now she was *really* confused. Say what you will about the perverse nut-job sitting in front of her, all his odious actions could be traced back to his scary patriotism. "But . . . but . . . but . . ." But that would mean that he had other motives. It would mean that maybe Stacy was in his life for reasons that had nothing to do with her. It would mean . . .

It *couldn't* mean.

"You're not her type," she said at last. "Her type is college football players and Oceanaire waiters."

"Ah, the Oceanaire. Her favorite restaurant. That woman can eat thirty raw oysters in five minutes, did you know? And then . . . what she does afterward . . . let's just say it's a good thing I've stayed in shape over the years."

Caitlyn realized, in despair, that the nanobytes would not let her vomit. Instead, she put her hands over her eyes and sagged into a chair. "Oh, God. Please kill me right now."

"Nonsense," the arse said briskly. "You're much too expensive to be struck dead by the wrath of God. Frankly, I'm amazed you weren't struck dead by the wrath of the Wolf. Now, what are you doing here other than trying to bribe me to break your best friend's heart?"

"Don't flatter yourself. Her heart wouldn't have broken. It wouldn't have even been bruised. I'm looking for Dmitri. He's not in our—I mean, he's not at the suite anymore. When I woke up, he—never mind. And his laptop's gone. I thought he might be here, looking for clues again."

The Boss shrugged. "I'm afraid there's not much to look for now. Dr. Miller's body is gone and the room has been processed."

"You know, people are dropping like flies all around you. Death could be lurking around the corner for any one of us."

"Yes, I know," he said absently, flipping through

the files on his desk. "I'm sure the situation is in good hands with you and the Wolf."

"You are not!"

"Caitlyn, go away. Go find the Wolf and solve my murder and save the world, and get me some coffee while you're at it. Oh, and if you see Stacy this afternoon, tell her she forgot her razor at my place."

Caitlyn gagged, and fled.

Chapter 33

Caitlyn stormed out . . . and nearly knocked Dmitri down. He cut off her apology with a kiss, swinging her off her feet and pressing her to him for a long hug. "Huh," she said when he finally put her down. "Someone's in a vastly better mood."

"Sadly, you're in the exact same mood you were when we left this place earlier," he teased, tugging on a hank of her hair. "Blue streaks?"

"I felt the need for a change."

"I've never met anyone with hair attention deficit disorder before."

"Oh, shut up. That's what they tell me at my salon. That reminds me, what's your favorite color?"

"The color of your eyes."

"Oh." That was kind of sweet. And to think, she'd been considering going to purple contact lenses one of these days. "Well, I'm not sure I can get the streaks exactly right. . . ."

"A weighty problem for another day. So, share

the bad news. Which of your friends has he started sleeping with now?"

"God, don't even go there. Where the heck have you been?"

"I have some preliminary data. Did you know Dr. Roe was the state pistol champion six years ago?"

"Uh, no. No, that little factoid must have escaped me. Good with a gun, huh?"

"Extremely good."

"Well, let's throw the book at her."

He quirked a small smile at her. "I doubt it will be quite that simple."

"Fine, whatever. Listen, you were gone when I woke up." She pouted. "I hate that."

"I do apologize. I was doing some research on Dr. Roe, and you looked so angelic, sleeping in my bed, I didn't have the heart to disturb you."

"Hmf," she said, mollified. "Well, what are you doing here?"

"A twofold reason: sharing my findings with Gregory Hamlin and—what's the phrase?—hooking up with you."

"Oh," she said, further mollified. "How'd you know I was here?"

"I picked you up on my long-distance scans."

"What? You mean you can find me but I can't ever find you?"

"Apparently not," he said cheerfully.

"No fair! You're gonna teach me how to do that too."

"Certainly."

"And I'm not going back into that office. I promised Stacy I wouldn't fold, spindle, or mutilate *him*."

He laughed. "Best not to try your word too quickly. Will you wait for me?"

"Sure." She glanced around the secretary's office. "I wonder where his assistant is? No matter what time I'm here, she's here too."

"She's doubtless a price beyond rubies. Wait for me," he said, pressing a kiss to her forehead and then disappearing into the Boss's lair.

"Stay alive no matter what occurs," she announced to the empty room. "I will find you." Best movie *ever*. Although, when Daniel Day-Lewis was making out with Madeleine Stowe and all that black hair was flying around, it was hard to tell who was who. . . .

She paced around the secretary's office area, again idly wondering where the über-efficient Rebecca had gone to. It was past lunchtime but too early for quitting time.

Bored, she went behind the desk, looking for candy and maybe a quick game of computer solitaire, and saw Rebecca's day planner was sitting right in the middle of her desk calendar.

It's none of my business, she reminded herself, eyeing the black leather cover.

Right. And minding their own business is something O.S.F. is soooooo good at.

So I want to be rotten like them? Besides, what difference does it make where she is? She's not your secretary.

No difference. But something's bugging me . . . niggling at the back of my brain, and I hate that feeling. . . . Why isn't she here? Isn't her boss in the middle of a crisis? So where the hell is she?

Sneaking a guilty glance over her shoulder, she picked up the planner and flipped it open. Glancing through the pages ("Order flowers for T.B." "Lunch with Miller" "Mom's birthday"), she found today's date.

There it was: 2:45 P.M. "Check on Dr. Roe."

"Oh, fuck," she said, dropping the planner.

Chapter 34

Rebecca tapped on the door, shifting the Burger King bag under one arm. The door opened and she nearly shrieked . . . she was staring down the barrel of a pistol.

"Dr. Roe, it's me! Rebecca, from the Boss's office!" She cowered in front of the barrel. "He sent me over to get your lunch order! Please don't shoot!"

Before she could back away, an arm shot out, grabbed her, and hauled her inside. The door slammed and she leaned against it, panting.

"You're carrying a Burger King bag," the be-spectacled, dark-haired Dr. Roe said suspiciously. Poor Dr. Roe! She looked quite stressed, with blood-shot eyes and wearing yesterday's clothes still. But the hands steadying the pistol (still in her face, Rebecca couldn't help but notice with increasing alarm) weren't shaky at all. "How can you be here to get my lunch order?"

"That's *my* lunch. You know how it is around

there. . . . I eat when I can. Um, Dr. Roe, could you please put the gun down? Actually, I was sort of wondering . . . where did you even get a gun?"

"Never mind," Roe grunted.

"I didn't know you had a . . . a pistol? Revolver? Whatever that thing is."

"It's a thirty-eight snub-nosed revolver, and I don't have *a* pistol, I have *three* pistols."

A deepening feeling of unease settled over Rebecca. "Um, okay. Well, I guess if it makes you feel safer . . ."

Dr. Roe threw back her head and laughed, laughed without enjoyment or humor. "Safer! Everyone on the team is dead. Except me."

"Yes, but the Boss is taking every precaution—"

"The Boss! I told him to put everyone in P.C. after Dr. Tanglen was killed. He ignored me."

"Oh, but it's not what you're thinking! He needed all of you—um, I mean, the rest of you—on the floor since Mirage was in the field. If something had happened to her or she needed help, the best team to help her—"

"Would be the team that made her."

"Well, yes. He couldn't—he couldn't just leave Mirage out there on her own."

"And never mind that it left us all open to be shot in the chest," Dr. Roe said bitterly. "He risked us to keep an eye on *her*. The sorority slut."

Rebecca stared. "How—how did you know they were—um—shot in the chest?"

Dr. Roe shrugged. "I'm team lead. I know everything."

With growing fear Rebecca eyed the taller woman. Dr. Roe was formidable during the best of times, her with her no-nonsense haircut and Anne Klein wardrobe and brutal, bitter outlook on life. She usually wore dark suits beneath her white lab coat and did not suffer fools gladly. But now . . . now, with her back against the wall, she was . . . was . . .

What?

"So the Boss sent you to get my lunch, huh? Terrific. I could use some empty calories. Suppose the son of a bitch would mind if I starved to death in protective custody?"

"You've got him all wrong," Rebecca protested, trying to back up but remembering, too late, that the door was closed behind her. "He works so hard . . . looks after all of us. . . ."

"Drives us like cattle, you mean. Christ, and to think I was excited when he revived the Wagner project. . . ."

"It made all your careers!"

"It made us all live at the lab. What home life? And for what? To cybernetically enhance that twit, that . . . that sorority chick, Caitlyn James. What a waste of six billion dollars."

"But the advances you made—"

"Aren't going to be common knowledge in my lifetime . . . any of our lifetimes. All that work . . . and for what?"

"Your work was good enough to win a Nobel Prize," Rebecca said, shocked. "You've revolutionized technology with your nanobytes."

"Yeah, too bad the O.S.F. won't let me talk about my work just yet. And I know what 'just yet' means, you know. It means 'it's going to be classified forever, no hard feelings.' "

"For the good of the country," Rebecca added.

"My ass," Dr. Roe replied rudely. "For the good of the Boss."

"I didn't know . . . didn't know this kind of thing was so important to you."

"I'll never be published," Dr. Roe said gloomily. "I thought I could get around that eventually, but the Boss won't let precious Caitlyn be endangered."

"Because he cares—"

Dr. Roe shoved her pistol in the pocket of her lab coat and glared. "My God, you're too loyal to be believed. I thought if anyone knew what a crumb the Boss was, you would."

"He's not a crumb. He's a fine man, a patriot. You just don't appreciate him. None of you appreciates him. The time the Wagner project takes away from him . . . why, he's devoted his entire life to the O.S.F.!"

"And for what?" Dr. Roe asked rudely. "So the latest product of the Wagner team can *not* work for us?"

"He saved her life. If we hadn't taken her on, Caitlyn would be dead. She'll realize that. She'll come around."

"You're nuts," Dr. Roe said, fingering the butt of her .38. "The whole thing was a waste . . . and now people are dead."

"That's true enough," Rebecca agreed with a nervous laugh.

Chapter 35

Dmitri stepped over the dead security guards without breaking stride, but Caitlyn couldn't stifle her groan of horror. It was bad enough the men were dead, but scattered in the hallway like this, left sprawling like dolls a cruel child didn't bother to put away . . .

Dmitri glanced back over his shoulder. "Steady," he said kindly enough, but she could only look at him and shake her head.

With a sinking feeling she scanned the guards, because Dmitri would have stopped if there had been any hope. They had been brain dead for some time.

"Goddammit," the Boss spat out.

"There's one life sign in the room," Caitlyn whispered. "But it's . . . it's . . ."

Dmitri kicked the door down and entered the room, Caitlyn and the Boss right behind him. She looked around wildly and saw the crumpled figure by the coffee table.

The room looked exactly like an apartment living room, complete with furniture and knickknacks. She didn't know what she'd been expecting . . . a motel room perhaps? She didn't know what protective custody looked like. What it looked like was an ordinary town house in Minneapolis. One filled with dead people. And why was she thinking about town houses and dead people right now?

So she wouldn't have to think about the poor lady on the carpet in front of her. The poor, shot—

Wait a minute.

"She's alive," Dmitri announced, bending over her. "Barely."

"There's an ambulance right behind us," the Boss said. "Move over. What happened?"

"Love," Dr. Roe croaked, blood bubbling down the side of her mouth.

"What?" The Boss and Caitlyn spoke in unison; Caitlyn couldn't hide her shock. They had come here to save Rebecca. But it wasn't Rebecca who had multiple gunshot wounds in her chest. It was—

"She did it for love," Dr. Roe said. "She told me. Gun in the Burger King bag. Put mine in my pocket. Stupid. Stupid. Never thought . . . thought it was about love . . ." Dr. Roe laughed, a dreadful choking cackling that made Caitlyn want to put her hands over her ears and scream *Stop laughing!*

"Where is she now?" Dmitri asked, taking Dr. Roe's hand and holding it gently.

"It was about love . . . and so she left. Caitlyn . . ."

"What about Caitlyn?" Dmitri demanded, his grip tightening.

". . . Caitlyn's house . . . going there for love . . . for *love*, have you ever heard anything so stupid?"

She laughed again, then her eyes rolled up and she quit laughing.

"Love," Caitlyn repeated, more shocked than she'd ever been in her life. "Stacy's staying at my house." Her eyes widened as all the pieces fell into place. Then she turned and ran.

Chapter 36

"**I** don't think you should drive," the Boss said through gritted teeth, clutching his seat belt. "Ever."

"Shut up. I've lived in that apartment for three years. I know all the shortcuts." She down-shifted and took the corner in third gear. "That bitch, that psycho! I don't care if she's the best secretary you ever had—if she shoots Stacy in the chest, it's gonna wreck my week."

"Drive faster," the Boss croaked, struggling to sit up after they'd turned the corner.

Caitlyn obliged.

The three of them stood on the west side of the building, looking up.

"That's it," Caitlyn said, counting. "Fourth one up."

"You can do it," Dmitri said. "Just calculate the angle plus the distance, and jump."

She stared at him. "Hi, we've never met. I'm Caitlyn."

"Just *jump*," the Boss said.

"What am I, trapped in an episode of *The Bionic Woman?* I couldn't even climb the rope in gym class."

"Caitlyn, *shut up*. Do it now. And one of you pick me up and take me with you."

"I think not," Dmitri sniffed.

"Do as you're told," the Boss ordered. "Now pick me up!"

"Don't look at me," Caitlyn said, because they were both doing exactly that when they weren't glaring at each other. "I don't know if I can do this by myself, much less with a passenger."

Dmitri sighed and slung the Boss into his arms like the world's biggest, meanest, scowlingest baby. "Watch me." Then he crouched, and shot straight up as if he'd been fired from a cannon. He went up . . . ten feet, twenty, thirty . . . ducked his head, sailed right over the railing, and landed on her balcony.

"Show-off," Caitlyn muttered, and crouched and jumped.

And knew immediately she'd screwed it up. She was going too fast, too high, she was going to sail right over her balcony and land on the fifth floor, maybe the sixth . . . and, frankly, she had to admit that if there was going to be a problem with her jump, she didn't think it would be *this* problem.

She made a wild clutch and grabbed the railing of the fifth-floor balcony. She hung there for a moment, legs dangling, then let go and dropped, and made another grab, and then she was holding on to the metal railing of her balcony, sliding down.

The Boss was staring at her and then grabbing

for her wrists, grabbing and tugging and grunting, and between that and her kicking and climbing, in another few seconds she was standing on the right balcony.

"You're welcome," the Boss panted.

"Shut up."

"I've got her," Dmitri said, ignoring her and the Boss's touching moment. "She's in the living room, talking to another female . . . I assume it's Stacy . . . and your balcony door is locked from the inside."

"So we'll break it," Caitlyn said. "Maybe the noise will distract her. Fuck the security deposit."

"On three," Dmitri said, raising his leg. "One . . . two . . ."

"It was so nice of you to stop by," Stacy said, "but Caitlyn's not here. And you know, she doesn't think much of the O.S.F."

"I'm aware," Rebecca said dryly.

"So, while I appreciate your coming by and all, maybe you should go before she comes back."

"I plan to be long gone before she comes back." Rebecca fumbled in her bag. "In fact—"

There was a tremendous crash, startling in the small apartment, and Stacy let out a small shriek. Then Caitlyn and Dmitri burst through—*through!*—the balcony doors. Glass was flying everywhere, sliding all over the kitchen tile, and for a second Caitlyn actually slipped, arms pinwheeling, and Stacy was sure she was going to go down, probably cutting the shit out of her knees, but Dmitri grabbed her arm and hauled her back up, and then behind them came Gregory!

"What the hell?" she started to ask her guest, Rebecca, the nice gal who worked for Gregory, but then Caitlyn was scooping up a handful of glass and . . . was she? She totally was! She *threw* the glass at poor Rebecca, who shrieked and started pawing at her face and dropped her Burger King bag, which hit the floor with a queer thump.

Stacy, more than a little shocked by the recent turn of events, bent to help Rebecca, poor Rebecca, who had blood all over her face, and a piece of glass was actually sticking out of her cheek, and Stacy said, "Somebody call an ambulance!" and held out her hands, and Rebecca clawed for her Burger King bag—odd time for a Whopper—and then—

She could see *everything*. Things had to be happening fast, *must* be, but she could see it all as if everyone were moving in slow motion, and had a bolt of thought, there and gone again like lightning: *This must be what it's like to be Jimmy! To see everything all the time!*

Because now Dmitri had picked up Gregory by the back of his shirt and the back of his pants and *threw* him, yes, tossed him like a tiddlywink, and Gregory flew through the air with the greatest of ease (for the second time that day) and just as he was passing in front of her, there was a *zim, zim,* a sound she did not recognize, and then Gregory was falling back against her and Caitlyn was there, right there, shoving Rebecca away, shoving her away so hard, the poor girl smacked into the wall and slid to the floor in a boneless heap.

The gun fell out of Rebecca's hand and Stacy saw the barrel had a queer swelling, had a thought *(a silencer?)* that was gone too quickly for her to grasp. She clutched Gregory, understood too late, and pulled his head into her lap.

"What'd you do?" she cried. "You idiot, what did you do?"

"I'll tell you this much," Gregory said, looking annoyed at the way the blood was seeping through his shirt and spreading across his chest. "I'm definitely going to let her go."

"Will somebody please tell me just *what the hell is going on*?"

"Well," Caitlyn said, looking puzzled and relieved and cute all at once (those blue highlights were so stoked!), "I guess the three of us just saved the day."

"Are you all right?" Dmitri asked, kneeling beside them.

"No, you Lithuanian moron, I'm shot," the Boss said irritably.

"I was speaking to *Stacy*," Dmitri corrected the Boss. "Are you?"

"No, I'm not all right! You guys broke Jimmy's door and Rebecca showed up with a gun and a Whopper—I think she has a Whopper—and now Gregory's shot and we were supposed to go out to Manny's tonight! What the *fuck*?"

"She's all right," Caitlyn said, carefully picking up Rebecca's gun, the expression on her face exactly as if she were picking up a dead tarantula.

"When I said 'get me over there,' " Gregory bitched to Dmitri through gritted teeth, "I didn't mean for you to throw me."

"Well, I couldn't teleport you," Dmitri said reasonably. "Lie still. You've got one in the left shoulder and one about two inches below that, but your heart is fine and your lungs are intact."

"Yeah, ya big baby," Caitlyn said heartlessly. Then, "Do you feel like you're dying? Do you see a light? Go into the light. Do you hear me? *Go into the light*."

"You're fired too," Gregory groaned.

"You can't fire me, I don't work for you," Caitlyn said.

"All the same," he snapped.

"I just don't understand any of this," Stacy cried.

"Yeah, it was kind of a mystery to us too. By the way, Stacy, the next time a multiple murderer shows up at my front door, I'd appreciate it if you didn't let her in."

"But . . . but I knew her! She's Gregory's secretary! She—"

"She did it for love. And she could get into anyplace in the O.S.F., including the labs, because she had clearance. Clearance I gave her, more's the pity," Gregory sighed, then groaned again when Stacy whipped off her scarf and pressed it to the bleeding wounds. "Ah, darling . . . hurts so good."

Caitlyn had an odd look on her face, one Dmitri saw as well, because he quickly took the gun away from her.

"Somebody's gonna tell me what's going on, right?" Stacy cried. "I mean, you guys aren't gonna keep me in the dark, right?"

They told her. Then she made them tell it again.

But she still didn't believe it.

Chapter 37

Later that night Stacy went back to the O.S.F., showed her driver's license, and was immediately buzzed up to Gregory's room. It was a pleasant surprise—she'd assumed with recent events that security would be more obnoxious than usual, and had doubts whether she would even get in. But Gregory must have left instructions. The big sweetie.

She had assumed he would go to the nearest hospital, but apparently the O.S.F. took care of their own, and had a whole wing full of hospital equipment and beds and doctors and stuff.

She found his room, finally, tapped on his door, and poked her head inside. When she saw he was alone, she stepped inside and shut the door behind her.

"A sight for sore eyes," Gregory sighed happily. "And sore chest."

"Just sore, huh?"

"Let's just say, tonight morphine is my friend."

He smiled at her. "I was hoping you would come by."

"Yeah?" She unbuttoned her knee-length rain-coat and shrugged out of it, putting her hands on her hips and striking a seductive pose. "Whaddya think?"

Gregory laughed until he choked. She was wearing what she thought of as Halloween costume circa 2001, or Slutty Nurse in White Fishnets.

"I think you should spend the night. That's what I think."

"Forget it, pal. Tonight you're just looking. No touching." She crossed the room and perched on the side of his bed, careful to avoid the many tubes poking out of him. "Gregory, you were nuts to get shot for me."

"I'm fine, thanks for asking."

"Oh, hush up. Next time just yell 'duck' or something. Okay?"

His fingers tightened around her own. "I couldn't let her hurt you."

"You idiot," she said, pressing a kiss to his eyebrow. "That's the coolest, most romantic thing ever, but I'm still pissed at you."

"You dressed up in that charming outfit and snuck in here to see me—"

"I didn't exactly sneak," she pointed out.

"—when you're pissed? I should annoy you more often."

"I'm sure you will."

"Come here. Lie down beside me."

"Uh, Gregory, I'm not sure . . ." She eyed the beeping machines and the tubes.

"Come here, I said."

"But what if it hurts?"

"What if it does?"

She cuddled in next to him and they were quiet for a long moment. Then he said, "I had my temp call Manny's. They're delivering a prime rib to Caitlyn's house this minute. I assumed you'd be there."

"Bitch is gonna eat my steak," Stacy grumbled. "Actually, I think she's shacking up in Mr. Yummypants's suite at the Marriott."

Gregory laughed, then gasped in pain. "His name is Dmitri Novakov."

"Whatever."

"But I think I'll start referring to him as Yummypants. That should annoy him nicely."

"See, this is why people don't like you."

"How about you, dear?"

"Oh, I like you fine," she assured him. "I know there's a heart under there . . . somewhere."

"Hmph," he mumbled. Then, "Don't forget. I warned you to be prepared."

"You really think Jimmy's gonna go with this guy? Back to the Baltic Sea or wherever?"

"I'm positive. Lithuania, BTW."

"Whatever. It's just . . . I mean, I know she likes him, but I didn't know she, like, *liked* him liked him. You know?"

"The horrifying thing is, I understood exactly what you said."

"Oh, knock it off. Well, if she wants to go, then God bless her. She's been alone for too long. Maybe I can get her apartment," she mused. "It's way nicer than mine."

"I know the feeling," he said quietly.

"I assume you're talking about being alone, not rent control. Yeah. Alone . . . boy, people do nutty things to avoid it. I still can't believe this—this mess is because Rebecca thought she was in love with you. I mean, I figured it'd be some super-secret-spy thing, not . . . you know. Thwarted love. It's just so *Days of Our Lives*, doncha think?"

"Please," he said. "Let's not talk about it. I'm finding the whole thing extremely embarrassing."

"Oh, quitcher whining."

"I *am* the one who's shot," he pointed out.

"I mean, she offed the Wagner team—everybody but the last one, right?"

"Not for lack of trying. But Dr. Roe will live. Not that she seems especially happy about it. She's still sulking because I won't let her publish."

"Yeah, but you explained all that to her . . . about how it'd be dangerous to Jimmy and Yummypants. Right?"

"Right. But Dr. Roe has . . . um, other considerations."

"Bitch. Even if she did almost die, she's still a bitch."

"Well said."

"Anyway, like I was saying, Rebecca did all that bad shit because she thought making Caitlyn was too hard on you. That you were working too many hours. I mean, I think you work a lot of hours too, and wish you'd take it easy, but I'm not gonna, like, kill everyone around you to get you to take a break."

"Thank you."

"I must not really love you," she teased.

"I'll keep working on you."

She kissed him again, this time on the nose. "That's a date, partner."

"There's plenty of room on this bed for two," he said hopefully.

"Forget it. I'll sleep on that couch in the corner . . . it's a convertible, right?"

"Brought up," he sighed happily, "just in case you needed it."

"Dude, you're, like, super-scary sometimes."

"I know."

Stacy was silent for a moment, musing, then said, "I guess it's a good thing that Jimmy was being, y'-know, Jimmy. Because her refusing to work for you worked out totally great for Rebecca, but she still had to stop the Wagner team from making any more like Jimmy. But then you totally shocked her by starting to go out with me, so she decided to ace me out of the picture too."

"Her mistake," Gregory said coolly.

"Man, the whole thing is just . . . sad and fucked-up, you know? What a mess."

"And a waste."

"At least you're okay."

"Not yet," he said, gripping her chin and pulling her in for a kiss, "but I will be."

Chapter 38

"I still hate him."

"Of course you do, darling."

"I'm serious!"

"So am I."

"Okay, so he took a couple of bullets for my best friend. That was almost . . . cool. Okay, it *was* cool. But one nice thing doesn't erase all the crummy things he's done."

"Certainly not."

"And I didn't check on him because I was, you know, *concerned* or anything. It was for Stacy's sake. Obviously, she's gone insane, but until she regains her senses, it's probably good if the creep doesn't die of blood loss or whatever."

"Quite right."

"Argh!" Caitlyn cried, throwing herself facedown on the bed. "My world has turned upside down!"

Dmitri was shutting down his laptop and smirking in her general direction. "Do tell."

"What, do tell? Haven't you been paying attention?"

"I'd like to hear your summation."

"I mean, how *weird* is all this? Stacy's going out with the nut, and he actually seems like he doesn't exactly hate her, which boggles the mind. . . ."

"Mm-hmm . . ."

"I mean, he took bullets for her. Who *does* that?"

"I would do that," Dmitri said quietly.

"I wouldn't have thought he'd take bullets for his granny, assuming he had one and wasn't, you know, spawned by the devil. Which I haven't entirely ruled out." Caitlyn flopped over and stared at the ceiling. "And all of this . . . it was because Rebecca was *in love* with him. Him! Is it possible the Boss is more attractive than I think he is? Naw," she said before Dmitri could answer. "I can't believe Rebecca thought he was working too hard and decided, in the manner of all psychos, to help him out. Does it surprise me that he had a slobbering nut-job working for him? No. Does it surprise me that she actually had *feelings* for him? Yup."

"At least we solved it," he said. "And your friend is okay, which is the important thing."

"That's true."

"And Gregory Hamlin is in the hospital with various tubes in his chest."

Caitlyn perked up. "That's true too. Tough for him to interfere in my life when he's flat on his back. And who knows? Maybe he'll have a really mean nurse."

Dmitri slapped the laptop closed and came over to the bed. "We can always hope," he said, bending to her. "I like your skirt."

"Thanks. Of course, I didn't think I'd be leaping balconies and such when I put it on." She smoothed the black pleats.

He pulled her shoes off, her socks, then reached under her skirt and relieved her of her panties. "You know," she griped, "I'm kind of having a crisis here."

"I know the exact cure," he assured her, rolling her over on her stomach.

"Men," she grumbled, then sucked in her breath as she felt him kneel behind her, pull her up on her knees, and then kiss her. Not on the mouth.

His tongue darted and licked while his thumbs held her open for him, and she rocked against his busy, busy mouth, forgetting her woes for the moment.

"God, you're so good at that," she groaned, biting her forearm.

He hummed in response, the vibrations doing delicious things to her tender flesh, and then she felt his tongue dart inside her and she trembled so hard, the bed shook.

After a torturous, delightfully long time when he wouldn't let her come and laughed at her when she begged, she heard his zipper come down, felt him slide his hand down her spine, and then he was easing into her from behind, and she pushed back against him, feeling him slam all the way home.

"Like that," she gasped.

"Yes," he replied, his voice so thick, she could barely understand the word.

He thrust into her, and she rocked back, and that was it, that was enough, she tipped over into orgasm and heard him gasp behind her, as if he could feel her all-over tightening. Their rhythm quickened, the bed slammed against the wall, and she reached between her thighs and found his testicles, warm and plum-sized, and cupped them in her hand, testing their weight, and he groaned and stiffened behind her.

They collapsed to the bed together. Caitlyn realized she still had her shirt and cardigan on, and her skirt, and Dmitri was fully dressed, just . . . disheveled.

"I think," he said after a long moment, "yes. I think you're going to kill me."

"*Me?* You're the one who's going for, like, the Boinking Championship."

He snorted against her shoulder, then flopped over when she elbowed him off her. "We're definitely going to hurt each other one of these days," she groaned.

"At least your archenemy won't be making love with your friend for quite a while."

"Okay, that's it. I'm never having sex again. No, really," she said as he started to laugh. "That little comment totally killed my drive."

"I'll see if I can revive it," he said, pulling her against him so they were cuddling together on the big bed. "Later. After a long nap."

There was a long, comfortable silence, broken when she finally asked the question that had been on her mind for the last three days. "Dmitri . . ."

"Um?" He sounded sleepy and content, and she almost hated to get into it. But it was better to *know*, dammit. No matter how much it was going to hurt. After all, the guy was probably getting on a jet as soon as his nap was over.

She asked, "Dmitri, do you believe in love at first sight?"

"No," he replied comfortably.

"Oh," she said, trying to ignore the stab of disappointment. "Yeah. That's what I figured."

"Do you?"

"What? Oh, no. No! Not at all."

"I don't believe in love at first sight because I loved you before I even met you," he explained.

"Yeah, that's what I—what?"

"What's that charming phrase you used? 'The nanobytes in your ears take the day off, or what?' " Her fist thumped lightly into his shoulder, and he grunted. "When my sources told me the Wagner team was reactivated, had created another cybernetically enhanced individual, I broke through their fire walls and security system and finally downloaded your file. I memorized it instantly, of course."

"Of course," she replied, flattered yet mildly creeped out.

"Some of the transcripts of your meetings with Gregory Hamlin were in there . . . and your reaction when you woke up in the hospital . . . your refusal to work for Hamlin . . . yes," he finished with a happy sigh, "by the time I finished your file, I was definitely in love."

"Dmitri . . ." She rolled over and kissed him. "That's, honest to God, the sweetest thing ever."

"What about you?"

"Oh, I fell in love with you when you beat me on the treadmill."

"So when I'm old and weak, you won't love me anymore?"

"I dunno," she said cheerfully. "I guess we'll find out."

"You plan to be around when I'm decrepit?"

"Well, duh. Boy. You're, like, the smartest guy and the dumbest guy, all at the same time. I mean, hello, I have been *totally* throwing myself at you."

"When you weren't sending me away and refusing to sleep with me," he pointed out.

"Jeez, how long are you going to hold that against me? I swear. Men are the biggest babies. Sulk much?"

He hugged her to his chest. "I'm planning on holding it against you for at least sixty years."

"Great," she grumbled.

"Come back to the castle with me."

"Sure, as long as you put in central heating."

"It's a national landmark," he complained. Then, "Really? You'll come?"

"You sound surprised."

"Well, I didn't think it would be that easy."

"I'm not letting some Lithuanian slut get her mitts on you. Frankly, it's sort of a miracle someone hasn't snapped you up before now. Not just because you're gorgeous. You're smart and cool and funny and, you know, neat and stuff."

He looked immensely gratified. "Most people find me . . . cold, I suppose. Nobody's ever . . . I mean, you're the first—"

"Well, 'most people' are idiots."

"*You're* the miracle. You're the one I was waiting for. Even if I didn't know it."

"Well, aren't you nice. Listen, I don't mind going back home with you, but I'm not living in Lithuania twenty-four/seven. I've got a business to run. In fact, I've neglected it shamefully lately. My clients all probably have split ends by now."

"I have three homes in the States," he replied. "It's no trouble to buy one here in Minneapolis."

"Oh. Right. Well, okay, then."

"But we will be married there, of course."

"As long as you fly Stacy over for it. And the gang from Tau Delta Nu. Lame proposal, by the way. 'We'll be married.' Boom. Dmitri has spoken."

"I'm sorry, I get bossy when I'm anxious, as my mother will be the first to tell you. My mother . . ." He trailed off, musing. "My, won't she be surprised."

"I'll bet. Well, she'll probably take it better now that she knows I'm not the killer."

"Indeed. Perhaps being a duchess will make up for my clumsy marriage proposal."

"Get out!" she cried, sitting up. "Are you *shitting*? You're a duke?"

"Didn't you read the file on me?" he complained.

"Yes, I read the file! I wish people would quit bugging me about the fucking file! There's nothing in there about being a duke."

"Well, maybe I didn't mention it to anyone in the O.S.F. when I was here."

"Yeah, *maybe*, you sneaky fuck. Duchess," she mused. "I'll have to, you know, get some duchess clothes."

"Your clothes are fine."

"And duchess shoes. And I need a manicure like you would *not* believe." She peeked at her fingernails, appalled.

"While we're on the subject of necessities, are we going to let Stacy bring a guest?" he teased.

"*God*, no."

"As you wish."

"Seriously, Dmitri. She can't bring a date. *No way*. I'm not having that—that—I'm not having *him* at my wedding. Forget it!"

"Great minds," he sighed, bringing her back into his embrace, "truly do think alike."

And here is a bonus story,
"Ten Little Idiots,"
by MaryJanice Davidson
that appeared in the anthology
"WICKED" WOMEN WHODUNIT
featuring a heroine with the
same moxie as Caitlyn James.

Prologue

Dana Gunn said, "I did it in the dining room with the candlestick."

She certainly didn't have to tell us, Caro Swenson thought. *And why do I feel like an extra on the set of CLUE instead of a vacationing nurse? "Professor Plum did it on the drawing room with . . ." Fer Christ's sake.*

The killer, a pleasant-looking blonde with curly Orphan Annie hair and big blue eyes, didn't have to make the announcement, because Caro could see for herself . . . the killer was standing in the hallway outside the bedrooms, calm as a cotton ball, the big candlestick in her fist actually dripping with the victim's blood.

Caro was a nurse, and long used to gore that would send a layman running for the toilet, but the cool way the killer held the weapon, the monotonous plink-plink of the blood hitting the carpet . . . it was startling, to say the least.

"Are you kidding?" Caro finally asked.

"I've already called the police," the killer declared,

dropping the candlestick, which hit the carpet with a thick thud and rolled a few feet away. She rubbed her bloody palm on the skirt of her Anne Taylor knockoff, grimaced like Lady Macbeth, then continued. "I'm just going to wait here in my room until they get here." Then she stepped backward and shut the door in Caro's face.

After a long, thunderstruck moment, Caro turned to the other guests and said, "I don't know about you guys, but this wasn't in *my* brochure."

Chapter 1

"This is all Jeannie Desjardin's fault," Caro declared to the people in the hallway.

Lynn Myers blinked at her. "Who-who's Jeannie Desjardin?"

"My friend. She's this awesomely horrible woman who generally revels in being bad. You know—she's one of those New York publishing types. But every once in a while she gets an attack of the guilts and tries to do something nice. Her husband and I try to talk her out of it, but . . . anyway, this was supposed to be *her* Maine getaway. But she gave me the tickets instead and stayed in New York to roast along with eight million other people." *And the yummy, luscious Steven McCord,* Caro thought rebelliously. *That lucky bitch.* "And now *look,*" she said, resisting the urge to kick the bloody candlestick. "Look at this mess. Wait until I tell her being nice backfired again."

"Well," Lynn said, blinking faster—Caro suspected

it was a nervous tic—"we should—I mean—we should call the—the police. Right?"

Caro studied Lynn, a slender woman so tall she hunched to hide it, a woman whose darting gray eyes swam behind magnified lenses. She was the only one of the group dressed in full makeup, pantyhose, and heels. She had told Caro during the first "Get Acquainted" brunch that she was a realtor from California. If so, she was the most uptight Californian Caro had ever seen. Not to mention the most uptight realtor.

"Call the police?" she asked at last. "Sure. But I think a few things might have escaped your notice."

"Like the fact that the storm's cut us off from the mainland," Todd Opitz suggested, puffing away on his eighth cigarette in fifteen minutes.

"Secondhand smoke kills," Lynn's Goth teenage daughter, Jana, sniffed. She was a tiny brunette with wildly curly dark hair, large dark eyes edged in kohl (making her look not unlike an edgy raccoon), and a pierced nostril. "See, Mom? I told you this would be lame."

"Jana . . ."

"And secondhand smoke *kills,*" the teen added.

"I hope so," was Todd's cold reply. He was an Ichabod Crane of a man, towering over all of them and looking down his long nose, which was often obscured by cigarette smoke. He tossed a lank of dark blond hair out of his eyes, puffed, and added, "I really do. Go watch *Romper Room,* willya?"

"Chil*dren,*" Caro said. "Focus, please. Dana's in there holed up waiting for *les flic* to land. Meantime, who'd she kill?"

"What?" Lynn asked.

"Well, who's dead? Obviously it's not one of us.

Who's missing?" Caro started counting on her fingers. "I think there's . . . what? Maybe a dozen of us, including staff? Well, four of us—five, if you count Dana—are accounted for. But there's a few of us missing."

The four of them looked around the narrow hallway, as if they expected the missing guests to pop out any second.

"Right. So, let's go see if we can find the dead person."

"Wh-why?" Lynn asked.

"Duh, Mom," Jana sniffed.

"Because they might not be dead," Caro explained patiently. "There's an old saying: 'A bloody candlestick does not a dead guy make,' or however it goes."

Jana was startled out of her sullen-teen routine. "Where the hell did *you* grow up?"

"Language, Jana. But—but the police?"

"Get it through your head," Todd said, not unkindly. "Nobody's riding to the rescue. You saw the Weather Channel . . . before the power went out, anyway. This is an island, a private island—"

"Enjoy the idyllic splendor of nature from your own solitary island off the Maine coast," Lynn quoted obediently from the brochure.

"Don't do that; it creeps me out when you do that."

"I have a photographic memory," she explained proudly.

"Congratufuckinglations. Anyway," Todd finished, lighting up yet another fresh cigarette, "the earliest the cops can get here is after the storm clears, probably sometime tomorrow morning."

"But they have helicopters—"

As if making Todd's point, a crack of lightning

lit up the windows, followed by the hollow boom of thunder, so loud it seemed to shake the mansion walls. The group pressed closer to each other for a brief moment and then, as if embarrassed at their unwilling intimacy, pulled back.

"They won't fly in this weather. We're stuck. Killer in the bedroom, no cops, power's out. The perfect Maine getaway," Todd added mockingly.

"It's like one of those bad horror movies," Caro commented.

"Caro's right."

"About the horror movies?"

He shook his head. "Let's go see who's dead. I mean, what's the alternative? It beats huddling in our rooms waiting for the lights to come back on, don'cha think?"

"What he said," Caro said, and they started off.

Chapter 2

"**D**id you used to be a Boy Scout?" Caro asked Todd, who was briskly handing out large flashlights.

"No. When you're a smoker, you get to know the lay of the land pretty quickly."

"Secondhand smoke—" Jana cut herself off as the blond man glared down at her.

"*Anyway,*" he continued, "when you have to sneak around to take your cigarette breaks because the entire fucking world has gone crazy over cigarettes—don't start, you guys, I *know* it's bad for me; nothing that feels so good could ever be healthy—you get to know the place you're staying at pretty well. I found this little pantry the first hour I was here."

When they all had flashlights—with working batteries, for a change—Caro set off, and after a moment the others fell into step beside her. She had given up her vacation as ruined, but setting that aside, she had an urgent need to find Dana's victim. Sure, there had been blood, but the human body could lose a lot of it and still live to play poker the next day. She had seen it.

"First thing, we find who Dana clocked with the candlestick," Caro said, leading them down yet another long, carpeted hallway. She could hear rain beating against the windows and followed the signs to the main dining salon. "See if he—or she—is okay."

"You're a nurse, right?" Lynn asked.

"Uh-huh. Maybe I can do something."

"Raise the dead?" Jana muttered.

Caro ignored that, pushed through the double doors to the dining room, and immediately shivered. All the windows against the far wall were open, as were the French doors leading to the large balcony where they'd had a pleasant lunch—was it only eight hours ago?

"Then we try to figure out how come."

"How come what?" Lynn asked.

"Well, why did Dana kill whoever-it-is? She must have had a reason, unless she's a sociopath. And she didn't strike me that way at lunch. And—eesh, this is megacreepy."

White curtains billowed and plumed out from the windows, and another crack of lightning lit up the room. Caro hurried through the doors—

"Careful!" Todd said sharply. "Don't slip."

—and skidded to a halt right before the waist-high stone railing. She looked over . . . and nearly fell herself.

"There!" she said, pointing with her flashlight. "Down on the rocks! Oh, Jesus, what a fall . . ."

The others crowded around her, their flashlight beams poking like long white fingers. Far, far below, a body was washed up on the rocks. It was so far below, and so battered by the waves, it was impossible to tell if it was even a man or a woman. The head was so tiny, you couldn't tell the length of hair or even the color of the hair—the rain could have made a blonde brunette, could have made a brunette more of a brunette, could have made a redhead mud-colored.

The setting sun set a bloody, broody glow over everything through the clouds, the perfect horrible creepy touch—not that one was needed.

"Oh, my God," Lynn peeped.

About the only thing she could tell for sure was—

"Well, that poor bastard's deader than shit," Todd declared.

"Very helpful," Jana said acidly.

"Oh, why don't you go try to put this place on the market? That's what you do, right?"

"I'm the realtor," Lynn said. "Jana works in a CD store."

"Well, go listen to Trent Reznor's latest, then."

"Quit it, children," Caro said absently. "Why is he—or she?—naked?"

Jana shuddered. "I don't even want to think about it."

"Why would Dana undress the victim?" Caro said to herself.

"To keep us from knowing if it's a man or woman?" Lynn ventured.

"Maybe . . . but why?" Caro frowned and stepped back from the railing. "Why let us know she killed them, but not tell us who it was? I mean, pardon my French, but what the *fuck?"*

"She's a model. That's what she said at lunch earlier, right? Well. They're capable of anything." Todd shuddered. *"Anything."*

Caro ignored the sarcasm. "Boy, there's just no way to get down there without breaking our necks, is there?"

"Get *down* there?" Jana's wild curls were plastered to her head in the driving rain, and she had to shout to be heard over the thunder. "Get *down* there? Have you lost your mind? We're not cops! I vote we all go back to our rooms and wait for the police to get here and take Dana back to the mainland."

"Yeah," Lynn added with a mighty sniff. She dashed rain out of her eyes and looked away from the body.

"Forget that," Todd said. "Just leave that poor schmuck down there on the rocks all night? For the birds and the fish and the—the whoever to do—you know. How'd you like it if it was you? Besides, he—she—they might be alive."

Caro didn't say anything. She certainly wasn't going to argue with him, although his initial assessment had been correct: whomever-it-was was deader than shit. Not that she was going to take that road . . . she and Todd were on the same page—she wanted to get to the body. Skulking in her room waiting for rescue didn't exactly appeal. She wasn't happy to be in the middle of this, but by God, she was *in* it.

"Look at this," she said, pointing. There was blood on the stone railing, blood that trailed all the way back into the dining room. "That's Dana, carrying the candlestick. She clocked this poor guy, shoved him—or her—over, then walked back to her room."

"Naked," Lynn added. "Shoved them naked."

"Barf out," Jana said with a grimace.

"Then *told* us she did it," Todd added. "In the

movies, the killer usually tries to, you know, cover up."

"She forgot to leave the candlestick behind—shock, probably," Caro continued, picturing it. "Didn't even remember holding it until she was talking to us. That's why there's a trail of blood."

"How handy for us," Todd said, trying unsuccessfully to light a new cigarette in the downpour. "Explains the blood in the hallway, too, huh, Sherlock?"

"Are you smoking those things, or eating them?"

"Hey, I'm stressed, all right?" he snapped back. "This isn't exactly my idea of a luxurious Maine getaway."

"What, it's *ours*? I could be in Minnesota right now, fishing on a lake."

"I could be in wine country," Lynn said mournfully.

"I could be indulging in minor property damage with my friends," Jana sighed.

"Aw, shaddup, you guys. Be nice or I won't tell you where the boathouse is."

"The boat—"

"I had a cigarette there earlier."

"Where haven't you had a cigarette?" Jana snapped. "Your lungs must look like a couple of pieces of beef jerky."

"Aw, shaddup. Look," he said, turning back to Caro, "we could take the little outboard, maybe try to rescue the—maybe try to get the body. Or whatever."

"Forget it," Jana said.

"Fine. Stay here. Alooooone," Todd said, wiggling his brows in a meaningfully scary way. "Hopefully

Dana won't come out of her room and decide to decorate your head with another candlestick."

They stared at each other in the rain. Nobody consulted Lynn, but then, why start now?

Mother and daughter exchanged a look. Then, "So, where's this boathouse?" Jana asked, resigned.

Chapter 3

". . . just through here . . . a little bit farther . . ."

"That's what you said ten minutes ago," Caro pointed out.

"Well, we're getting close."

Under ordinary conditions—which was to say, when they weren't looking for a dead body in the steadily deepening dark, worried about the killer up at the mansion and being lashed by torrents of rain—this was probably a pleasant little path to the boathouse.

Not so much right now.

"It's just down there," Todd said, pointing. "See?"

They could see a small, squat building with a green roof just at the end of the path, and beyond that, a river gurgled alongside. Caro guessed the river must lead directly to the sea, and they could take the boat around to the back of the mansion, fish the body out, and then . . .

What?

She'd worry about that later.

"Is there a reason we aren't leaving this to the owner of the mansion?" Lynn ventured, stumbling in her pumps.

"He might be the dead guy," Caro replied. "And it's a big place. He could be anywhere. Heck, he could have gone back to the mainland after supper for all we know. I don't want to waste time looking for someone we don't even know is alive. I'd rather get to the victim."

"It's touching, yet a little on the creepy side," Todd said. "I'm sure it has nothing to do with your obsessive need to be in charge."

"Here we—ow! Son of a bitch!" Jana cursed and shoved the branches out of her face.

"Jana!" her mother gasped. "Watch your mouth."

"That probably stings like crazy," Todd commented, smothering a snicker.

"Does anyone know how to drive a boat?" Lynn asked timidly.

"I can do it," Caro said. "I used to go fishing with my old man on the Mississippi all the time."

"Aw, that's so cute," Todd said. "And when I say cute, I mean lame. Uh-oh."

Caro didn't ask what uh-oh meant. She and the others had reached the door to the boathouse . . . and the lock was smashed and hanging open.

"Dana's smarter than I thought," Todd said. "And that's really saying something—didn't she say she was a teacher?"

"What's so dumb about that?"

"She teaches modeling."

"Her evil knows no bounds," Caro said. "And she knows a few other things, too." Caro poked at the broken hasp. "Well, let's go see how bad it is."

She pushed the door open with tented fingers

and walked in. Part of her couldn't believe this was happening to her, would-be author and pediatric nurse. Tramping around in the dark, in a spooky damp boathouse where she could barely see her hand in front of her face. Followed by the three musketeers: Larry, Moe, and Curly. Oh, Lord, what a day. *Next time,* she told herself grimly, *stay home or stay in bed. Possibly both.*

She took a deep breath and went in a little farther, feeling like every stupid horror movie heroine ever conceived. She could practically hear people yelling at the screen, "Don't go in there, dumb bitch!"

She kept her flashlight trained in front of her, which was why she didn't see the body at her feet and went sprawling.

"Ouch," Todd said, looking down at her. "That looked embarrassing."

Chapter 4

Caro scrambled back, away from the body. She could feel wet muck sliding down her shorts and didn't care. Wet snakes could be sliding down her shorts and she wouldn't care. The body on the floor . . . she cared about *that*.

"Oh, gross!" Jana cried.

"Another body," Lynn gasped.

"Dana's been a busy girl," Todd said. "Where's my lighter?"

"You dropped it on my back," the body said, rolling over and sitting up. The four of them screamed in unison. "Ow! Not so loud . . . my head . . ."

"You're alive!" Caro blurted. It was the first thing they taught in her nursing courses: determine if your patient is living or dead.

"Unfortunately, yes." The body rubbed the back of his head and squinted up at all of them. "Hey, thanks for coming to get me, you guys. I thought I was a goner when she nailed me."

He got to his feet with some care, then bent,

winced, and helped Caro to her feet. She couldn't help staring at him. He was mussed and muddy and a little pale from the blow to his head, but for all that, yummy besides.

He was dressed in dark blue boat shoes and black swimming trunks, and nothing else. The mat of hair on his chest was dark and curly, the hair on his head a lighter color with streaks of gold, and his eyes were—she squinted in the gloom—dark green . . . almost exactly the color of the wet leaves all over the boathouse floor. She'd never seen eyes that color before.

"You're not a dead body!" Caro said again, because she honestly couldn't think of what else to say to him.

"I'm Turner."

"Last name Turner or first name Turner?"

"Just Turner."

"Like just Kramer on 'Seinfeld,' " Jana said helpfully.

"No, Kramer's first name was Cosmo," Todd said. To Turner, "I remember you. Breakfast, right?"

"Yup."

"Like Madonna, then," Jana was babbling.

"Or Cher," Lynn added.

"You guys, could we stay focused?" Caro demanded. "Turner's not the dead body. In fact, who *are* you? I didn't see you at lunch."

"Oh, I work here. Give tours, run the tourists down the river to some of those riverside restaurants . . . kind of an all around go-to guy."

"Oooh, ooh," Todd said, grinning. "Stop it."

The body quirked an eyebrow at him, then continued. "I came down here when the storm started kickin' up to make sure the boathouse was locked up, when—holy crap—you'll never guess—"

"Dana smashed the lock, damaged the boat, hit you over the head with something, came back told us what happened, and locked herself in."

Turner was gaping at them. "Well, shit. There goes my story. Figured it was good for a couple of beers at least. Not to mention, you guys know more of what happened than I do."

"I'll buy you a beer anyway," Lynn said.

"I got here in time to hear her rummaging in the boat and got my 'guests aren't supposed to use the boats unless I'm with them' lecture ready, when everything went dark and I went night-night. Didn't even see her coming." He rubbed the back of his head and winced. "Girl's got a swing like a Major Leaguer, I'll tell you that much."

"That's interesting," Todd said.

"Interesting as in psychotic? Interesting as in laughable? What are we talking about? Help me out."

"Well, you're a big guy, a *very* big guy, pardon me for noticing, and Dana's at least a foot shorter than you. She would have had to swing *up*. She must have really wanted you out of her way."

"Or didn't like you."

"At least she didn't kill me, and believe me, this isn't the first weekend I've had to say that. Well, let's check the boat anyway."

They did, and Turner announced, "Even if she hadn't punched that hole in the stern, I don't see any spark plugs, do you?"

"What does one look like?" Lynn whispered in Caro's ear.

"Search me," she shrugged. "So Dana knows about engines, too. Okay."

"But . . . how come?" Jana ventured. "I mean, grody enough that she killed whoever, but why come down here and fix it so we couldn't get the body?"

"Probably the same reason she won't tell us who she killed," Caro said. "Question is, now what?"

"Now we go back up to the mansion and wait for the cops," Lynn declared. "We're soaked, it's getting late, it's *dark*—"

"Aw, Mom," Jana whined, stealing another glance at Turner's legs.

"—and there's a body bobbing around the water somewhere . . ." Lynn shuddered.

Turner looked puzzled. "Well, who is it?"

"That's what we're trying to figure out," Caro explained. "Obviously, it's not you. And there's a few more of us missing. Four or five at least. We don't know who she killed . . . or even if she's done killing."

"Well, shit! Let's find out!"

"It's so nice to have a man in charge," Todd murmured, taking a deep drag.

Caro giggled. "Want me to look at that?" she asked, indicating the lump Turner kept rubbing.

"Naw. Got worse than this from my mama. Let's try to round up the others, make sure they're all okay."

"There aren't that many more of us," Caro reminded them. "Stop me if you've heard this, but . . . who the hell did she kill? And *why*?"

"I can get the list of guests from the register, and we can go from there."

"What a great idea!" Caro cried. "Shoot, we should have done something like that first."

"I thought you wanted to find the body first?" Todd asked.

"Well, now I've reprioritized. So, let's go get that list. You guys? Everybody game?"

"Okay," Jana and Lynn said at once. They both had identical expressions of hunger on their faces, which made them look more than ever like mother and daughter. Caro supposed they just needed the right incentive to be socially conscious. The right, six-foot, three-inch incentive.

Caro and Todd rolled their eyes. "All right, then," Caro said. "Let's go."

Chapter 5

"You know, you should go for it," Todd told her. They were trudging back up to the mansion/resort/hellhole, rain beating down on them like a live, malevolent thing. Todd and Caro were trailing behind the group. Jana and Lynn hovered so close to Turner, they were practically holding his hands. "I saw the way you looked at his butt."

"I was not," she said, jerking her gaze higher. "What are you talking about?"

"Oh, come on. You like him, I can tell."

"Todd," she said patiently, "I don't *know* him. Or you. Can we stay focused, please? Heck, a few minutes ago I thought he was a dead body."

"The only impediment to your budding romance, I might add. Make a pass. He'll be receptive, I bet. A little va-va-voom on your vacation, do you good."

"Todd! We're sort of in the middle of something, here. There's a time and a place, and this ain't it."

"Details," Todd grumbled.

"Why don't *you* make a pass, you think it's such a great idea?"

"Oh, believe me, I did. Right after breakfast. Hello, you see his pecs? Oofta. Alas, he politely turned me down." Todd sighed, then brightened. "But I bet he wouldn't turn *you* down." He squinted at her in the rain. "I bet your hair is past your waist when you get it out of that tacky braid. And it's probably not usually muddy and brownish."

"It's blond," she said, stung.

"Well, drowned rat is *not* a good look for you, darling. And you're almost as tall as he is. Actually . . ."

"That's enough."

". . . you've got sort of the forties starlet thing going, with your teeny waist and big boobs."

"That's the nicest thing anyone's ever said to me," she said sarcastically. "Now shut your face."

"Except for the glasses," he added heartlessly. "Big purple frames? In *this* decade? You should lose them and try contacts."

"I hate contacts. They itch my eyeballs. Can we please stop this?"

"But it's why you came here. It's why we all came here."

"That's not true!" she cried.

"Oh, sure it is," Todd went on cheerfully. "Not necessarily to hook up—like an island Love Boat, how lame would that be? And who does that make me? Doc? *Gopher?* But to be with people."

"I'm here only because my friend was too busy to go and she gave me her tickets."

"Okay," he said. "But why did you *come?*"

"It doesn't matter," she snapped.

"I'm just saying." Todd looked at the fresh cigarette and tucked it away without bothering to try to light it in the downpour. "You should ask him out. I bet he's into you. God knows he wasn't into *me.*"

"And who could resist you?"

"Exactly."

Caro grinned in spite of herself. "You're an asshole, Todd."

"Exactly."

Chapter 6

"Okay," Turner said as they all dripped across the lobby. The mansion had such a large foyer, it was used as a check-in area. He went behind the large mahogany desk, rummaged around, and produced a printout. "Here's the guest list for the weekend. Everybody on the island is on this. There's—"

"What do you think you're doing?"

"Aaiigghh!" they all cried, including Turner, who straightened so fast he clutched his head. Todd actually jumped behind Caro.

They all spun around to look. The manager of the resort was blinking at them from the doorway leading to the kitchen. He was dressed in a tan linen suit and looked like a sleepy Colonel Sanders with his closely trimmed beard and short white hair. His eyes were very blue as he stared at them. "Why are you yelling? And isn't it getting a little late for all this charging around? I was just about to retire for the night. And why are you all wet? Do you know what these carpets cost?"

"That's the owner guy," Jana said suddenly. "He checked us in this morning."

"I remember, miss. Richard Calque," he said. "What's going on?"

"Rich, you'll never believe this," Turner said. "One of the guests is dead. I'm glad it's not you. Best boss I ever had," he added in a mutter to Lynn, who had sidled over to him.

"Dana killed him . . . remember from lunch? Short, red curly hair, wicked swing? And locked herself in and won't come out."

"What?"

"I know, I know," Caro said. "But it's true."

"But who is dead?" Richard asked, looking bewildered.

"That's just it. We don't know. I mean, we know it's not you," Caro said, "and we know it's not Turner. We came up here to get the names of the other guests. We figured we'd track them down and make sure they're okay."

"But the police—"

"Aren't coming. Not for a while, anyway. Stupid private island," Todd mumbled. "*Seemed* like a good idea at the time . . ."

"But there is a police officer among the guests," Rich said.

"Get out of town!" Caro hadn't expected some *good* news, not the way things had been going so far. "Really? Who is it?"

"Okay," Turner said as Caro, overcome with curiosity, went to him and read over his shoulder. "We got Dana . . . check. We got Jana."

"Check," Jana said, dimpling.

Caro glared at the teenager while Turner continued. "We got Lynn, we got Caro, we got Todd. We got me, we got the boss."

"Please," Rich said modestly, flicking an invisible speck off his spotless sleeve. "Call me Rich."

"That leaves the honeymooners—"

"Right, and the husband's a Brit," Todd added. "Great shoes."

"I remember," Lynn said excitedly. "Not the shoes, but I remember because they looked so odd together . . . he's this big strapping fellow, and she's this little tiny elfin thing; but he's a little starchy, and she's got this amazing foul mouth. They disappeared after lunch." Lynn colored. "You know, honeymoon business."

"The cook, Anna Barkmeier—"

"Room eight," Caro said, still shamelessly reading over Turner's (broad) shoulder.

"And that's it," Turner said, looking around at all of them. "Ten of us."

"What about the rest of the staff? There's, like, fifteen bedrooms in this place. There must be more than this."

"With only seven guests, I really only need two other people to help me run the mansion," Rich said mildly. "I haven't been the owner very long . . . it's a bit of an experiment."

"Keep owning it," Turner ordered.

"If dead people keep showing up, I'll likely sell as soon as possible and go see what my niece and nephew-by-marriage are up to," Rich retorted. "How do we know this person is dead, by the way?"

"They're dead," Todd and Caro said in unison.

"Well, I hope it's not one of the honeymooners," Turner said. "They seem like they're really in love

and happy. I don't want to tell either one of them
that the *other* one is dead."

"So let's go find them," Caro said.

Corinne Bullwinkle Daniels was on the brink of
a truly profound . . . revelation . . . when someone
started hammering at their door.

"Ignore it," her husband, Grant, panted beneath
her.

"Way ahead of you," she gasped back, but the
pounding, if anything, speeded up. Followed by
the shrieking.

Her husband cursed as she climbed off him, then
cursed more when she tossed a blanket over him,
shrugged into her robe, and yanked the door open.
"What?"

"You're alive!" the stunning blonde answered.
She was wet, muddy, and completely bedraggled . . .
and looked better that way than Corinne had looked
on her wedding day. Not *too* annoying. "That's so
great!"

"Thanks. We don't need any towels. Good-bye,"
she said, starting to swing the door shut, but the
blonde stuck her foot out.

Corinne looked down at the foot, then looked
up—up, up!—at the tall woman. "Good way to get
a fracture, bee-yatch," she warned.

"Is your husband all right?" she asked, trying to
shove past Corinne.

"No, he's not all right, he's pissed off, and so am
I." Corinne started leaning on the door. "We're on
our honeymoon, fuck you very much, now *go away*."

"Pissed off," the owner said, peeking over the
blonde's shoulder, "as in, not dead?"

Corinne gave up, and the door swung open the rest of the way. Grant sat up and tucked the blanket demurely around himself. "What in the world is going on? Corinne, darling, let them in."

"Bad idea. Don't feed any of them," she said, stepping back, "or they'll never leave."

"We're dreadfully sorry to bother you, Mrs. Daniels—"

"Not as sorry as we are," Corinne grumped.

"But there's been . . . a murder."

Even though Rich said it with the appropriate dramatic pause, it was still hard to believe.

Corinne and Grant blinked at each other, then blinked at him. "There's been a *what?*" Corinne asked.

Quickly, the tall blonde—who would be breathtaking once she dried off and washed her hair, and her clothes—explained.

"Seriously?" Corinne asked when the blonde finished. "It's not a joke?"

"If it was, it would be in extremely poor taste. I understand you're a police officer," Rich said, "so if you could just—"

"Simmer down, Colonel Sanders," Corinne said, making the time-out motion with her hands. "One, I'm not a cop. I'm a private investigator—I quit the force when I got engaged."

"But—"

"Two, even if I *was* a cop, which, if you missed the memo, I'm not, this isn't my jurisdiction. In fact, we're about fifteen hundred miles from my jurisdiction."

"But—"

"Three, where's the killer?"

Their room was just *full* of people, Corinne saw

to her annoyance, and they all stared at each other and then gaped at her. *Oh, SUPER helpful.*

"In her room," the blond woman finally said. "She locked herself in a couple hours ago when she told us what she did."

"And she's *still* there?"

"Uh . . . I think so."

"Did you—is anybody guarding the door so she doesn't get away?"

"Uh . . ."

Civilians. Lord help us. "Mmm." Corinne grabbed a pile of clothes out of her suitcase and marched to the bathroom. "Nobody go anywhere," she ordered. "I'll be right out."

A short silence fell, while everyone in the room tried to look everywhere but at the obviously mussed Grant Daniels. (Everyone except Todd.) Finally, the blonde said, "My name's Caro. This is Turner, Jana, Lynn, Todd, and Rich."

"Grant Daniels," he said, shaking her damp hand. "So. Uh. How do you like Maine?"

"It's . . . exciting," Daniels said, eyeing the group with something close to wariness.

Chapter 7

The tiny Mrs. Daniels, who really did look like an elf with those short limbs and tip-tilted dark eyes, hammered on Dana's door. "Hey in there!" she shouted. The amount of volume pumped out by that tiny frame was startling, to put it mildly. "Are you okay?"

"Go away!" Dana shouted back.

"Who'd you kill?"

"Mind your own business!"

"I'll tell the cops you cooperated!" Corinne yelled into the keyhole. "And they'll tell the D.A.!"

"History will exonerate me!"

"History will *what* her?" Lynn asked.

"I'm telling my whole story to the press!" Dana shouted. "But I'm not coming out there until you can guarantee my safety!"

"*She's* scared of *us?*" Turner asked. "Oh, that's rich."

"What?" Rich asked.

"Never mind, boss."

"Okay," Corinne said, turning back to the group. "So at least we know she's still in there. I guess the murder weapon's in there with her."

"No," Caro said. "It's—oh, shit!"

"Don't tell me, let me guess." Corinne paused dramatically, then rolled her eyes. "It's *gone*. Bum-bum-*bum!*"

"Completely gone," Rich said, eyeing the bloody patch of carpet with distaste.

"It was *right there,*" Todd said, pointing. "Right there!"

"So she either came out to get it, or somebody took it."

"Who would take it?"

Corinne shook her head. "Okay, so the crime scene is totally fucked."

"Totally fucked?" her husband teased. "As opposed to only partially fucked?"

She ignored him. "We'll worry about that when the locals land. There's no way to properly process the scene anyway, not without the right equipment. It's too bad, because the more time that gets wasted . . . anyway, it's better to just leave the whole place alone and try to find out who's dead. Is there a way to lock her in?"

"Yes," Turner and Rich said in unison.

"So, let's do it."

Caro was impressed. She so rarely met a woman as forceful as herself. And this one was half her size! Bet she gave her husband hell on a regular basis. "Good idea."

"Uh . . . darling . . ."

"I know, Grant," Corrine replied, holding up her hands. "I'm not a big fan of squashing constitutional rights, either. Well, usually. Sometimes. But she admitted to murder. I think for everyone's safety, we lock her up until the cops come."

"Come on," Turner said, and to Caro's complete surprise, he grabbed her hand and pulled her away from the group. "I know where the keys are."

"That's nice," she said, unnerved by the pressure of his big hand around hers. "Are they so heavy you need help carrying them?"

"No. But I'll feel better if I know you're with me."

The evening was getting more surreal by the minute. Dead bodies she was used to—she worked in a Minneapolis emergency ward, for God's sake. Criminals she was used to—bad guys as well as good guys got sick. But scrumptious-looking handymen wanting to be with her? Being protective of her? That was just too damn weird.

"Uh . . . uh . . ."

"You know, I noticed you at breakfast."

"I didn't notice you," she confessed. "I was too busy listening to Mr. and Mrs. Daniels debate whether or not King George was a bad enough king to justify the Revolutionary War."

"Right."

"Apparently he wasn't such a bad guy."

"Right."

"I mean, to hear the British guy tell it."

"Right. Are you okay?"

"I'm a little nervous," she gasped.

"Oh, sure. Understandable. You know, with dead bodies and killers and ex-cops running around."

That's not why I'm nervous, buddy boy. "Uh-huh."

Turner was rummaging around behind the big desk, and then he emerged with an old-fashioned set of keys on a large metal ring. "Haven't seen something like this in a while, huh?" he asked her. "Amazing how fast we all got used to key cards. But this place is two hundred years old, and Rich refused to put modern locks on the doors."

"Uh-huh." *Oh, you're really impressing him with your wit and style! Good thing you don't LOOK LIKE HELL or you'd really be in trouble.* "That's . . . uh-huh."

"Listen, Caro," he said, fixing her with a look and then grabbing her hand again. "I want you to stay away from Dana."

That broke the spell. Thank goodness! "No shit. Thanks for the tip."

He had the grace to look abashed. "Well, it's probably tempting to talk to her, try to get some details, right? Tempting for you, I mean."

"Well . . . yeah . . ." *How does he know that?*

He grinned at her. "You seem like the curious type. But she's dangerous. Like, drooling crazy dangerous. Network-executive-run-amok dangerous. Steer clear. For my sake, okay?"

"Why in the world do you care?" She had to restrain herself from slapping her own forehead. *Oh, shit! That was out loud!*

"I just . . . do. I wouldn't want anything to happen to you." He rubbed the bump on his head. "She just knocked me cold, but that could have killed someone else. And I—I knew her. From before."

"Knew Dana?"

"Well, yeah. We sort of have a history. Not much of one," he added, seeing the alarmed look on Caro's face. "She was out here our opening weekend, and I—we—we sort of spent the night together. But she wouldn't have anything to do with me afterward." He shook his head. "My own fault. One-night stands never lead to anything good. Should have kept my pants on."

"I guess *so*." *Ya big pig*, she thought but didn't say.

"She was sort of—uh, she came on kind of strong. And I was kind of lonesome, and—look, I'm not proud of it, okay? I'm just saying, please stay away from her."

"Don't worry," Caro said. "But if I do get near her, I promise not to fall into bed with her."

He blushed. Blushed! Red to his eyebrows. "Look, I just wanted to tell you, okay?"

"How come? I mean, why me?"

He shrugged, looking uncomfortable. "I—I think you're kind of cool."

"You don't even know me," she said, flattered in spite of herself.

"No, but I'd like to. I noticed you earlier and tried to figure out how to talk to you, but you're so gorgeous and classy . . ." He trailed off.

"*I* am?" she practically gasped.

"I hate to say it, but as awful and scary as this whole thing is, it gave me a chance to, you know, talk to you."

Okay, this is getting weirder and weirder.

"Come on," he said. "Let's go lock her in."

Wordlessly, she let him lead her back to the others.

Chapter 8

"Why would she kill the cook?" Caro mused aloud, after Dana had been locked in her room. Turner had jammed a chair against the door-knob for good effect, and everyone had breathed easier. Now they were all in the small dining room where breakfast had been served earlier. Lit candles gave an appropriately spooky glow to everyone's face. "That's the only one we haven't found, right? The cook? Anna what's-her-name?"

"Barkmeier," Rich confirmed. "She's been in my employ for about a month. And I don't know why."

"You never heard them—Dana and the cook?—arguing about anything?" Corinne pressed. "About money, men, whatever?"

"No. Nothing. I barely saw Dana before she . . . you know."

"This might be kind of a dumb question," Turner said, "and it's off the subject, but has anyone tried their cell phone?"

"Yes," Todd and Caro said gloomily. Todd added, "The storm must have taken out the tower, or whatever cell phones have. Nobody can get a signal."

"And land lines are out, needless to say," Corinne observed.

"Right."

"Well, getting back to the subject, as a former cop, I can tell you, people kill other people for the dumbest reasons in the world . . . or no reason at all. I once arrested a guy who shot his wife because she burned the pork loin. Honest to God."

"Well, maybe Dana didn't like Anna's cooking," Todd said, trying to smile.

"Maybe Anna had something she wanted. Or did something she didn't like. Or knew a secret Dana didn't want to get out. Seriously, you guys, it could be anything."

"I just wish we could get her body," Caro said.

Corinne shook her head. "It's better you leave it where it is. The first commandment of crime is, Thou shalt not fuck up thy crime scene."

Grant snickered, then sobered when everyone looked at him. "Sorry. That was amusing to me."

"So . . . what?" Todd asked. "We're just going to sit here in the dark and stare at each other? Blurgh."

A short silence, followed by, "Well, there's really nothing we can do, right? Dana confessed, and we locked her in. We can't get the body—and shouldn't, anyway. We know who's dead. Everyone else is accounted for. And it's now . . ." Corinne grabbed her husband's wrist and squinted at his watch. "Eleven-thirty-two P.M. And the storm . . ." Another crash of thunder. "Isn't letting up anytime soon. And . . . frankly, you guys . . . I'm on my honeymoon, here."

"Darling, you're insatiable."

"Shut up, Grant. Anyway. I vote we all go back to our rooms and hit the sheets."

"That sounds all right," Lynn said cautiously. "I mean, I was against tromping around in the woods from the start. If there's really nothing more we can do . . ."

"I'll post watch outside Dana's door," Rich volunteered.

"I'll do it," Turner said, shooting a glance at Caro. "Maybe I could have some company?"

Caro opened her mouth, but Rich interrupted with, "No, no. It's my mansion, I'll do it."

"Okay, but then I'll relieve you at . . . what? Three o'clock?"

"That sounds fine, my boy." Rich rose, adjusted his pleats, and bowed. "Until tomorrow morning, then."

"Turner, will you walk me to my room?" Jana asked. "It's so dark . . . and scary . . . and you're so . . . big . . ."

"I can't," he said. "I promised Caro I'd . . . look at her JAMA collection."

"What?" Caro asked.

"JAMA?"

"Journal of the American Medical Association," Caro said automatically. Then, "Oh. Oh! Right. I've been dying to show you my, uh, collection."

Later, as they scampered down the hall like kids freed early for recess, Caro asked, "How in the world do you know about JAMA?"

"My sister's a doc," he replied easily. "Thanks for going along with it. Badly, I might add."

"Well, give a girl some warning next time!"

"How about this?" he asked, and pulled her into his arms and, right below the painting of the elderly woman with the flashing eyes and wispy moustache, kissed her.

Chapter 9

"Just so you know," Caro gasped, coming up for air, "I never do this."

"Me neither. Okay, I do it sometimes."

"You did it with Dana!"

"Believe me, that was *way* more her idea than mine. I thought she'd be there in the morning so I could buy her breakfast, maybe we could spend the weekend together, get to know each other, but . . ." He shook his head. "Gone."

"Oh, like that's the first time that's happened. You probably horndog after all the girl guests."

"No," he said soberly, pulling back and looking at her. "I don't."

They were in her room, and she couldn't help noticing it was just romantic as hell with the candles and the lit fireplace. How was a girl supposed to resist? Not to mention, Turner must have been a Boy Scout in his youth, because with the help of four matches and several pages from *US* magazine, he had a blaze going in no time.

They kissed again, hungrily, exploring each other's mouths, and she traced her fingers along his jawline and across his shoulders. He was as firm to the touch as he was candy to the eyes, and smelled delicious . . . if slightly damp.

His hands were busy beneath her BLO POP T-shirt, grazing the flesh just beneath her bra, big warm fingers sending shivers down her spine . . . the good kind of shivers, for a change.

"Seriously," she said again, breaking the kiss. "I mean, I *never* do stuff like this. When I'm not working, I'm writing. Doesn't leave a lot of time for a social life."

"You're a writer?"

"Would-be. I'm still trying to get published."

"Well, if you came out here for inspiration, you got it in spades."

"Are you talking about the murder?" she teased as he nibbled on her earlobe. "Or other things?"

"Mmmf," he replied, then pulled his lips away from her ear. "Uh, listen, Caro, I really like you . . ."

"Well, I didn't think that was a roll of Life Savers in your pocket."

"Life Savers?" he said, offended.

"Caro, I really like you . . . ," she prompted.

"That's about it. I mean, I wasn't really going anywhere with it."

"Very romantic," she grumbled. "As it happens, I like you, too, but don't ask me why. I mean, five hours ago, I didn't know you. This is *so* unlike me."

"You keep saying that," he murmured, kissing the base of her throat. "And then you keep doing things."

"The whole thing. Isn't like me, I mean. Oooh, that's nice, don't stop doing that."

"Don't worry."

"I don't even read mysteries, y'know? I'm strictly a cookbook girl. Well, and maybe a few Star Trek novels. I just love Commander Riker."

"Could you not reveal your major geekiness right now? It's sort of killing the mood."

"Give me a break. It's just so weird to be in the middle of all this. The last mystery I read was . . . I can't even remember. Miss Marple I'm not."

"Definitely not," he said, nuzzling her other ear. "I sort of liked the way you took charge."

"You weren't even there."

"Oh, Jana and Lynn were bitching about it."

"Figures," she snorted. "I doubt Jana's legal, by the way, so don't get any ideas."

He actually shuddered. "Don't worry. Neither of them is my type. She's too young, and her mom's too annoying."

"Nice way to talk about guests," she teased.

"And if this is all so unlike you, how come you're here?"

"Well . . . I'm just trying to be polite . . ." Her fingers brushed the front of his shorts. "And I did pack some condoms. It's been so long since I bought some," she added grumpily, "the pharmacist laughed his ass off."

He pulled away from her. "Oh. That's good . . . that's great. But I wasn't going to, y'know, push you or anything."

"You were quick enough to jump into bed with Dana!" she said, stung.

"*She* jumped in with me. I told you, the whole thing wasn't exactly my idea," he said patiently. "I don't want to wreck things with you. I mean, a one-night stand isn't exactly what I'm after. They don't work for me."

"Well, what are we doing here, then?"

His brow clouded. "Oh, I'm like your summer vacation boy toy? Bonk the help and then go back to the real world?"

"You're not the help," she said, shocked. Then she thought about it. "Well, I guess you are. But I didn't think about you that way. Honest."

"That's true," he said. "First you thought I was a dead body."

"But then you got better!"

He laughed. "Sorry. I guess I'm a little touchy. I felt really used by Dana, you know?"

"Sure, I can understand that."

"It's just, you're so classy and beautiful, I didn't think you'd even talk to me. And now that we're here . . . it's like it's too good to be true. I don't want anything to ruin it. You know, anything more than felony assault and homicide."

Classy and beautiful? Was he high? Was *she?* But he was right about the too good to be true part. The whole night had a definite surreal cast. Death and sex . . . whodathunkit?

She was right about one thing. This *wasn't* like her. But for once in her life, she was going to do something irresponsible and weird. And Turner was going to help!

"Anyway," she said, determined not to waste the opportunity, "about those condoms . . ."

There was a sudden rap at the door, and they both jumped. Then Caro laughed nervously. "Dum-dum-*dum!* I guess it's been that kind of night."

"I'll get it."

She pushed him back on the bed. "Stay put. And how about losing those shorts? It's my room, I'll get it." She crossed the room and called through the door, "It's not the killer, is it?"

"No," a confused-sounding female voice said from the other side. "I'm looking for Turner."

Caro opened the door and beheld a freckled, red-haired woman who was almost exactly her height. Her hair was sleek and damp, the color of strawberry pie, and she was barefoot and dressed in denim shorts and a red polo shirt. "Hi," she said, extending a large hand.

"Hi. Listen, you've found Turner, but you can't have him."

The redhead looked confused. "But I need him."

"Join the club, babe."

"No, I mean, he's supposed to help me with the garbage bins. I can't move them by myself, and I've got to prep for breakfast."

Caro stared. "Uh, why?"

The redhead stared back. "Because it's my job. I'm the cook? Anna Barkmeier?"

"Aigh!" Caro cried, and slammed the door shut.

Chapter 10

"What? What?" Turner was at her side in a second. "What's the matter?"

"It's the body!" she cried, leaning against the door. "The body is here, looking for you!"

"You mean *Anna?* Move." He jerked the door open. "Holy shit!"

"You slammed the door on me," the body complained, aggrieved. "I hate that."

Caro goggled. "You're not dead!"

Turner gave her a curious look. "That seems to be a thing with you. You're always shocked to find out someone's alive."

"No, I'm *not.* I mean, I am tonight, sure. But it's not 'a thing' with me. Not normally. Jeez, Anna Barkmeier! I can't believe it!"

"Anyway," the body continued doggedly, "if I could just borrow Turner for a few minutes . . ."

Turner grabbed her by the elbow and pulled her into the room. "Where the hell have you been?"

Anna tripped on the rug and nearly went sprawling, then jerked her elbow away and glared at them both. "I was stuck in town, of course. Miserable storm. Why, were you looking for me?"

"Actually, no. We thought you were—uh—it's a long story," Caro finished sheepishly.

"Well. Now I'm way behind on breakfast prep, so I really need you to—"

"But who's dead?"

"Corinne! Open up!" Caro hammered on the door. "We found the body!" Silence from inside the room. Caro hammered more. "I'm sorry to bother you again, but the body's here!"

Suddenly, the door was jerked open, and a disheveled, hastily robed Corinne stood there, glaring. *"You're* going to be the body if you don't quit interrupting us," she growled.

"I know, I know, I'm sorry. But the body came looking for Turner."

"The body did *what?"*

"For heaven's sake," she heard Grant say from inside the room. "Let her in, Corinne, or she'll beat on our door all night."

"I didn't know you were into that stuff," she snapped, then stepped back.

Embarrassed, Caro scuttled into the room. "Hi again," she said breathlessly as the scrumptious Grant, looking resigned, once again rearranged the covers over himself. "Sorry. I'm really sorry. But this is important."

"Oh, you always say that. 'Come quick, there's been a murder.' 'Come quick, we found a dead body . . . again.' " Grant smiled at her to take the sting out of his words. "Can't you come up with anything good?"

"Funny," she said. "But we really need you guys. See, Anna being alive poses kind of a problem."

"You got *that* right," Corinne replied. "For starters . . ."

Chapter 11

"**W**ho the hell is dead?"

"I—I don't understand," Anna said faintly. "What's going on? Why is everybody up? Have you filled out your breakfast orders?"

"Screw breakfast," Todd said. "We've sort of had a few other things on our mind tonight while you were slumming in town."

"I wasn't—"

"One of the guests killed somebody," Corinne explained. "We don't know who, because with you being alive, everyone's accounted for."

"But—but—who—?"

"Whom," Jana corrected loftily.

"Shut up, Punky Brewster," Todd ordered.

"Dana Gunn killed someone, then confessed and barricaded herself in her room," Caro said. "Before she did that, she conked Turner over the head and wrecked the boat so we couldn't get the body. Which is weird in itself . . . she confessed to murder but

us who she offed? What, like she's
Don't you guys think that's weird?"
awful night is weird," Lynn said.
Dana *killed* . . . ?" Anna rubbed her
temples, as if a sudden, throbbing headache had
appeared. Which, for all Caro knew, it had. "I don't
understand . . . and you thought I was . . . ?"

"Well, you were the only one we couldn't find,"
Jana said peevishly. "Thanks tons for disappearing,
by the way."

"I don't believe it," Anna muttered, still rubbing.
"I just don't believe it."

"Believe it, sis," Todd said, exhaling a cloud of
smoke and looking not unlike a sulky blond dragon.
"But you turning up begs the question . . . and stop
me if you've heard this before, but who'd she kill?"

"Whom did she kill," Jana corrected.

"And why?" Caro asked, ignoring the teen. "I
still want to know why."

"If you knew *why* she killed, you'd probably know
who," Corinne pointed out.

"This is decidedly freaky," Turner commented.
"Now what do we do?"

"The storm must be letting up," Grant said. "If
Anna was able to get back."

Corinne frowned. "Anybody try their cell phone
lately?"

"Why do you think I was stranded?" Anna snapped.
"My cell wasn't working, among other things."

"All right, all right, don't foam at the mouth. I
suggest we all go back to what we were doing—"

"Insatiable," Grant murmured.

"Works for me," Caro said cheerfully.

"—and we'll get together again when the police
are here."

"That sounds all right," Lynn said tentatively.

"Well, it's not like you've got a lot of choice. You'll all have to give statements, anyway."

"But I've got breakfast to get on with," Anna protested.

Corinne gave her a look, and the redhead subsided.

Chapter 12

"Well, if there's nothing else we can do . . ."
Her shirt went flying, followed by her bra.

"I'm a handyman and you're a nurse. We're not the police." His shorts joined her shirt on the floor, and then they tumbled to her bed. "Now, if they needed something repaired . . . or if someone needed a vaccine . . ."

"Then we'd be there for them. But they don't. And . . ."

"And we've got to pass the time somehow."

"Right!" She pulled the covers up over both of them and gasped with delight as he suckled her breasts.

"Or the minutes will just drag by . . ."

"And we can't have that!"

"Damn, you've got the best rack I've ever seen."

"That's so romantic," she sighed. "Ooooh, don't stop. That's wonderful."

"And your ass isn't bad, either."

"Turner, maybe you shouldn't talk while we do this."

He laughed, then abruptly sobered, which was startling. "Do you think we should be enjoying this? I mean . . . someone's dead."

"Yeah, but what can we do? I think we just established that we're mere observers."

"Good point." His hand slipped between her legs, and she wriggled against him. "Oh, God, you feel so sweet . . ."

"Just wait," she promised him. "I'll—"

There was an abrupt knock at the door, and they both froze.

"Hey in there!" Corinne called. "Let us in!"

"Fuck," Turner swore.

"No, we'd better not," Caro said, then called, "Just a minute!"

"Where'd you put my shorts?"

"Where'd you put my bra?"

Twenty seconds later, she was pulling the door open. "What?"

"Ha!" Corinne crowed, instantly analyzing their flushed faces.

"Shut up and come in already. What is it?"

"Terribly sorry to interrupt," Grant said, looking embarrassed. "But Corinne had some thoughts . . ."

"So?" Caro asked rudely.

"Well, there's a couple of things," Corinne said, kicking Caro's bra out of her way, marching across the room, and sitting on the bed. "Anna said she was stuck in town, right? And she said her cell phone doesn't work?"

"Right. So . . . ?"

"But ours does. We just called the locals, like five minutes ago."

"Well, maybe she's got a different service than we do . . . ," Turner said doubtfully.

"Right, anything's possible, but that *did* get me thinking. If she lied about her cell, maybe she lied about being stuck in town. And if she hasn't been stuck in town, what's she been doing?"

Caro's mouth popped open. She had just flashed back to seeing Anna standing outside her door, with wet hair and bare feet. And . . . there was something else, wasn't there? Something . . .

"She's tall," Caro said slowly. "But Dana's short. I remember being surprised when I saw Anna, because I hardly ever meet women as tall as me. But Turner got hit in a bad place . . . low, almost on the back of the neck. Dana would have had to swing up . . . but *Anna's* a big girl. She wouldn't have had any trouble conking him a good one."

Comprehension dawned on Turner's face. "So *Anna* went down to the boathouse, to prevent us from getting the body. And she probably took the bloody candlestick, too. But that means Dana . . ."

"Dana's been in her room the whole time," Caro said, feeling a definite chill race down her back. Bad enough the killer was in the house with them, but knowing Anna was scuttling around, covering things up for the killer and lying herself black in the face . . . that was fucking creepy. "Anna never went to town. She's been here all along, covering up for her . . . protecting her . . ."

"Because she *didn't know Dana had confessed!*" Corinne finished triumphantly. "That's why she looked so totally poleaxed earlier. Not because she was shocked about the murder . . . she was shocked that Dana had told us *she* was the killer! It made all the crap she's been doing totally unnecessary. No wonder she looked sick!"

"But . . . why?" Grant asked.

"Well," Corinne said, "let's go ask her."

Chapter 13

"I don't know what you're talking about," Anna said through tight lips, peeling potatoes so rapidly her hands were practically a blur. "Now that the power's back on, I'm way behind. Why don't you go back to your rooms?"

"Anna, you want to cut the shit? We *know*," Corinne said impatiently. "Your story doesn't hold water with us, and it sure as shit won't with the local cops, who, by the way, should be here in about ten minutes."

Caro nodded, and glanced around the large, spotless kitchen. Something was missing, but she couldn't quite put her finger on it. What was wrong? There was a small shelf full of pictures, but that wasn't it. Distracted, Caro stepped closer to the pictures. Family stuff, mostly, Anna posing in front of various gorgeous scenes . . . and one was flipped down.

"Not to mention, where are the groceries?" Corinne gestured at the large kitchen. "No damp bags, no extra food . . . because you never went to town."

That's what was wrong, Caro decided, fingering the turned-down photo. No food. Anna hadn't had time to return from shopping, put everything away, *and* find Turner. Because, of course, she had never been shopping. Heck, where could she go? Was there even a grocery store on the island? She supposed they could check the garage, see if Anna's car engine was warm. Another nail in the coffin.

"You'd better cough up the truth," Corinne went on relentlessly, "because it'll just be that much worse for you if you lie to the locals."

Caro flipped the picture back up, positioned it where it belonged, started to turn back to the group . . . then took another look at the picture.

"So why don't you just talk?" Corinne finished.

"Jesus Christ," Caro whispered, staring at the photo. Everything made sense . . . a horrible, skin-crawling sense. Poor Turner. Poor Anna. And poor . . .

"I don't know what you're talking about," Anna repeated stubbornly, peeled potatoes flying into the pot. "I didn't go to town for food, I went for . . . for . . ."

"You're covering up for Dana. By my count, you've destroyed property, tampered with a crime scene, and committed felony assault, and that's just for starters. The cops are going to want to talk to you. We'll make sure of that. So all this crap you pulled was basically for nothing. Why not tell us?"

Anna glared at Corinne, and her grip tightened on the potato peeler. Grant stepped protectively in front of his wife and got a poke between the shoulder blades for his pain. "Don't do that," she snapped, elbowing him out of the way. "On my slowest day, I could take her."

"Let's stop provoking unbelievably dangerous people, what do you say, dear?"

"Anna, won't you tell them why?" Caro had flipped the picture back down. For her, there were no more questions. But the others . . . Corinne was definitely on the right track. Anna looked as though she was going to puke. Or faint. Or both. "Why in the world would you do all this stuff? Steal crime scene evidence and hurt Turner?" Especially hurt Turner, who was only guilty of being in the wrong place at the wrong time, *both* times, poor dope. "What was it all for?"

"Yeah, we work together, Annie," Turner added. "You and me and Rich, we were making this place into a real weekend getaway for people." He rubbed his head and looked at her reproachfully. "I kind of thought we were a team."

"A team!" Anna spat. "Ha! *You're* the cause of all this, Turner, you ass."

"Me?" Turner gasped.

"*Him?*" Corinne gasped. "What'd he do?"

"You led her on, that's what. That whole 'studly handyman looking for love' nonsense you give off like . . . like pheromones."

"I'll admit he's cute," Grant said, "but I fail to see . . ."

"She's my sister," Anna said in a small voice. She put the potato peeler on the counter and stared at the floor.

Caro could practically hear the air being sucked out of the room as everyone gasped. "Dana's your *sister?*" Corinne managed, while Caro nodded tiredly.

"I didn't lead her on!" Turner protested. "*She* was all over *me.*"

"That's kind of a minor detail you could have mentioned," Corinne said. "The killer being, you know, *a blood relative* and all."

"Not just that," Caro added. "Isn't that right, Anna?"

"No, no. I mean, yes, she is, but she killed . . . our sister."

"The body's your sister, too?"

"I think I'm going to faint," Grant murmured.

Anna looked peeved. "Turner, you ass, don't you remember? I brought them both out here on opening weekend."

"Well, yeah, I remember Dana from before," he said slowly, "sure I did. But . . . nothing ever came of it, and I figured . . . I just figured she was here *this* weekend as a returning guest. Rich wants to build up repeat clientele, so I didn't think anything of it. I tried to be friendly, you know, talk to her, but she was totally cold to me. I guess she . . . I guess she didn't like me from before."

"That's not true," Caro said quietly.

Anna snorted. "Didn't think anything of it . . . that's you in a nutshell. And I suppose you don't remember Tina?"

He frowned. "Tina? No, I didn't meet her. I only met Dana."

"No, you met Tina *pretending* to be Dana."

"How could she pretend—"

"She had a crush on you. She would have done anything for you."

"Who are you talking about?" Grant asked.

"But I only talked to her for five minutes! I—"

"So your sister fixated on Turner," Corinne interrupted. "And it sounds like Dana did, too."

"But I didn't do anything!" Turner was looking more horrified by the second. "I was nice to her!"

"You slept with her!"

"No, I didn't! I didn't! I slept with Dana!"

"Somebody give me a notebook," Corinne muttered. "I'm gonna have to start writing this down to keep track. Who'd you sleep with, Turner?"

Anna ignored the interruption and went on in a tone that stung. "Tina wanted to see you again . . . and Dana did, too, only she didn't tell me." She looked at the floor again. "So I snuck Tina out here this weekend—"

"Which is why she's not on the registry," Grant observed.

"—but Dana didn't tell me she was coming, too, as a guest. And Tina . . . Tina was going to—well, I guess she was going to, what's the phrase, make a play for you? And Dana . . . she didn't like that."

"So Dana beaned her with a candlestick and threw her into the ocean?" Caro hoped she didn't look as horrified as she felt. She wanted Anna to keep talking.

"You know how sisters are," Caro continued dully. *"Sisters?"*

"As far back as I can remember, they competed for everything . . . fought to win everything. Toys. And when they were older, boys. And I guess Dana wasn't going to let Tina win this time."

"You mean Dana had a wicked sister?" Turner looked flabbergasted. "Or, wait a minute, Dana *was* the wicked sister? Christ, how complicated is this going to get?"

"Turner, I don't think you've . . ." Put it all together, Caro was going to add, but then, she had the benefit of the photo. Anna, standing with her sister, Dana. And someone who looked a lot like Dana.

"But that means . . . when I slept with Dana, her sister made up her mind to sleep with me, too?" Turner looked horrified. "I wouldn't have hurt Dana. But she must have thought—"

"And you tried to protect the sister who was still alive, right, Anna?" Corinne prompted.

"I saw it happen . . . I'd come down to the dining room to see if they wanted to go into town for supper. I was there to hear them fighting, rounded the corner in time to see what happened, but I wasn't in time to stop it. I've—I've never been able to stop them."

"Tina was found naked," Caro said softly, "because she was going to try to seduce Turner wasn't she? And that did it. Dana had had enough."

Anna nodded. "So I told Dana to lock herself in her room and not come out, and I—"

"Made yourself useful, covering up the crime."

"I didn't know she'd confessed," Anna said bitterly. "I thought if I could prevent any of you from finding the body—"

"And not noticing the way Tina looked exactly like Dana," Caro added dryly.

"—that I could get Dana away before anything—anything happened. But then Turner came snooping around, and none of you would stay in your rooms. And one of you turned out to be a cop, for goodness sake."

"Ex-cop," Grant and Corinne said in unison.

Anna raised her head and glared at Turner. "This is all your fault."

"Uh . . ." Caro held up a finger. "Actually, I think it might be all Dana's fault."

"Dana just wanted something—someone nice for herself, is that such a crime? She doesn't even think it's a crime, and if you knew how Tina taunted her . . . tormented her . . . all their lives . . . it's not really a crime, right? Wanting to be able to hang on to something nice, for once? Wanting something your sister can't have?"

"No, of course not," Corinne said, "but murder is."

"All this," Caro said, "for a crush? Because Tina pulled one over on Dana, and Dana wanted to get even? That doesn't make any sense!"

"No," Anna said. "All this because one of them had to be the winner. All the time."

Chapter 14

"I still don't believe it," Turner said, shaking his head. "Those poor girls."

"And poor Anna," Caro added. "One sister's dead, and the other's headed for prison. I know it wasn't too cool that she, you know, practically killed you, but I can't help but feel sorry for her."

He nodded. "No wonder Dana wouldn't tell us who she killed. How could she confess to killing her own sister? And over something so dumb? I'm serious, Caro, I barely knew the girl. *Girls.*" He shivered. "And here I slept with the killer . . . and now her sister's dead. God . . ."

"More of their sick games," Caro commented. "Like Anna said, in the end, it wasn't about you, or even love. It was about winning. You know what's the worst? That picture I saw, the one Anna kept in the kitchen. Of the three of them? None of them are smiling. They're someplace warm, on sand that looks like sugar, they're wearing tropical flowers around their necks . . . and none of them are smiling."

"Those poor girls," Turner said again.

There was a short silence, and then Caro, the night catching up with her, yawned. "Listen, we've got some time before . . . I mean, we're done talking to the cops and stuff . . ."

Turner looked at the bed, then looked at her. "Let's just lie down together, all right?"

"Very much extremely all right."

She crawled into the bed, noticing the sun was starting to come up over the horizon. Turner climbed in beside her, and they curled up like spoons in a drawer, and slept.

"All checked out, then?" Rich asked.

"We're ready to rock," Corinne said. The group had, by necessity, been forced to become close in an obscenely short amount of time, and now they found separating difficult. "Listen, you guys, if you're ever in Minneapolis . . ."

"I live there," Caro said, smiling.

". . . or San Diego," Lynn added.

". . . or Boston," Todd said.

"Well, I'm not telling any of *you* weirdos where *I* live," Jana huffed, snatching her bag away from Rich.

"But you live with me, dear," Lynn began.

"This was, like, the lamest vacation *ever.*" She glared at the group. "The absolute worst." She tossed her curls out of her face and stomped off.

"I'll miss that bitch," Todd sighed.

"I wouldn't go that far," Grant commented.

"All I can say is, I hope to God I can score some smokes on the way to the airport." He bent and kissed Caro on the cheek. "It's been real, blondie. And what that means, I have no idea." He hefted his bag and waved at the others. "Hope to see you all again. Under less interesting circumstances."

"Heck, I don't mind so much. It made me lonesome for the force," Corinne said. "I gotta admit, it was one for the books."

"Not much of a honeymoon for you two, though," Turner said.

"Oh, we'll get it right next time," Corinne said airily. She slung her duffel bag over one shoulder and sketched a salute. "Later, gators."

"Good-bye," Grant said, shaking hands all around, then followed his wife out the front door. "You know, darling, there's always the Mile High Club . . ."

"Well, 'bye," Lynn said, and hurried after them.

"You know, I don't think she said twenty words all weekend," Turner commented, watching her go.

"Yeah, but she's got a great story to tell when she gets home. And I've got a great story to write. Although," she added as Rich looked vaguely alarmed, "I will change the names to protect the innocent."

"Bad enough I'm short a cook," he grumbled. "That kind of publicity I do not need."

"You kidding?" Turner asked. "People will swarm to this place just to see where the candlestick got dropped . . . where poor Tina went over the rail. You could double your prices and they'd still come. People are weird."

"Ugh," Caro said. "The whole thing was a waste, if you ask me. Tina's dead . . . and for what? Dana's in jail, thinking she's the winner . . . for what? Over a guy they hardly knew, but decided to fight over. A guy who was a doll in their tug-of-war."

"Beats me," Turner said, looking honestly puzzled. "There's lots of guys out there."

Caro took another look at his tousled dark hair, his vivid green eyes, the long, tanned legs. Poor bastard. No clue how finger-lickin' good he really was.

"I hope we'll see you again, Caro," Rich said, shaking her hand.

"Next weekend?" Turner asked hopefully.

"Jeez, I really couldn't afford . . ."

"Oh, you'll stay as a guest of management, of course," Rich said. "It's the least I can do."

"Well," Caro said, stealing another peek at Turner, "maybe I will."

Epilogue

She arched her back to meet his thrusts and clutched his shoulders to bring him closer. He shuddered over her and bit her lightly on the ear, and her orgasm burst through her like a shooting star. Moments later he stiffened, went deeper than he had before, and then he collapsed over her.

"Oh, thank God," Turner groaned.

"Yeah, *finally*," Caro sighed.

"I'm glad you came. Uh, to visit again."

She giggled. "Me, too." He kissed her again and rolled away, and she sat up. "Although, I have to say, it's been extremely weird to be here and not worry about, you know, dead bodies."

He laughed and patted her leg. "It's not usually like that. Last month was the exception, big-time."

She snorted. "Prove it."

"I plan to."

She glanced at her watch. "Let's see . . . I've been here for an hour. How do you want to fill the rest of the weekend?"

"I'll need another ten minutes . . ."

"Not *that*. Although it's tempting. But don't you have work to do?"

"Don't you?"

She stared at him. "Oh, come on. You don't mean Rich was serious."

"You kidding? I bugged him about it constantly until you came back."

"You guys don't need a live-in nurse on the grounds."

"After what happened last time?" He rubbed the back of his head.

"You guys are serious?"

"Caro, get it through your head: we want you to stay here. *I* want you to stay here."

She was flattered, thrilled, and scared. All at the same time. Kind of like last month. "But we barely know each other."

"Look, you're right, it's definitely crazy, okay? But so what? I'll tell you what I *do* know; I thought about you constantly while you were gone. That month felt like a damn year."

"I missed you, too," she admitted.

"I want you to stay. Rich has a job for you. Give it a try," he coaxed. "There's worse things than hanging out on a gorgeous secluded island off the coast of Maine and trying to hurt each other, you know, sexually."

"I guess." She grinned. "I guess we could give it a try. If I survived what happened last month, I could try anything." She sobered. "But if I'm going to stay here with you, I have to know one thing."

"Anything."

"What's your full name? I can't just go around calling you 'Turner' all the time."

He grimaced. "I'll tell you, but you should know, only my mom and my sisters know it. You'll have to take an oath of secrecy."

She held up her hand, palm out. "I swear."

"Seriously. You can't tell anybody."

"I won't tell anybody."

"It's Fred."

"Fred?" She bit her tongue so she wouldn't laugh. Fred! Oh, that was a riot. "Well, that's . . . it's very . . . classic. Yes, it's a very old-fashioned, nice, classic name."

"I hate it," he said gloomily. "A Fred does your taxes for you. A Fred wears a tie and drinks cheap scotch."

"A Fred is giving me a whole new life," she said, stroking the tip of his ear with her finger.

He brightened. "That's true."

"So, it's not so bad. Not, you know, *murder* bad."

"That's true, too. You know, I'm sort of falling for you, here. You didn't go into gales of humiliating laughter when I told you my name. My mom always said the one girl who didn't laugh at my name was the girl for me."

"Your mom's pretty bright, then. Fred."

"No."

"What's wrong, Freddy?"

"No."

She glanced at her watch again. "So, is that ten minutes up yet?"

He pounced on her. "Close enough."

"I'm with you on that one . . . Fred."

If you missed MaryJanice Davidson's
wonderfully funny and sexy book
DOING IT RIGHT,
here's an excerpt.

Tap-tap-tap.

"What the hell *is* that?" he muttered, getting up and crossing the room. He had a flashback to one of his literature classes. "Who is that tapping, tapping at my chamber door?" he boomed, pulling back the curtain and expecting to see . . . he wasn't sure. A branch, rasping across the glass? A pigeon? Instead, he found himself gazing into a face ten inches from his own. "Aaiiggh!"

It was her. Crouched on the ledge, perfectly balanced on the balls of her feet, she had one small fist raised, doubtless ready to knock again. When she saw him, she gestured patiently to the lock. He dimly noticed she was dressed like a normal person instead of a burglar—navy leggings and a matching turtleneck—and wondered why she wasn't shivering with cold.

He groped for the latch, dry-mouthed with fear for her. They were three stories up! If she should lose her balance . . . if a gust of wind should come up . . .

The latch finally yielded to his fumbling fingers and he wrenched the window open, grabbing for her. She leaned back, out of the reach of his arms, and his heart stopped—actually stopped, ka-THUD!—in his chest. He backpedaled away from the window. "Okay, okay, sorry, didn't mean to startle you, now would you please get your ass in here?"

She raised her eyebrows at him and complied, swinging one leg over the ledge and stepping down into the room as lightly as a ballerina. He collapsed on the cot, clutching his chest. "Could you please not ever *ever* do that again?" he gasped. "Christ! My heart! What's going on? How'd you get up there? Did the nurses lock all the entrances again? They do that when they're overworked—"

"'Quoth the Raven, nevermore'," she said, and helped herself to a cup of coffee from the pot set up next to the window. At his surprised gape, she smiled a little and tapped her ear. "Thin glass. I heard you through the window. 'While I pondered, nearly napping, suddenly there came a rapping, rapping at my chamber door.' I think that's how it goes. Poe was high most of the time, so it's hard to tell. Also, the man you saw me bludgeon into unconsciousness dropped a dime on you today."

"He what?"

"Dropped a dime. Rolled you over. Put you out. Phoned you in. Wants to clock you. Wants to drop you. Made arrangements to have you killed, pronto. Sugar?"

"No thanks," he said numbly.

"I mean," she said patiently, "is there sugar?"

He pointed to the last locker on the left and thought to warn her too late. When she opened it (first wrapping her sleeve around her hand, he noticed, as she had with the coffee pot handle), several hundred tea bags, salt packets, and sugar cubes tumbled out, free of their overstuffed, poorly stacked boxes. She quickly stepped back, avoiding the rain of sweetener, then bent, picked a cube off the floor, blew on it, and dropped it into her cup. She shoved the locker door with her knee until it grudgingly shut, trapping a dozen or so tea bags and sugar packets in the bottom with a grinding sound that set his teeth on edge.

She went to the door, thumbed the lock with her sleeve, then came back and sat down at the rickety table opposite the cot. She took a tentative sip of her coffee and then another, not so tentative. He was impressed—the hospital coffee tasted like primeval mud, as it boiled and reboiled all day and night. "So that's the scoop," she said casually.

"You're here to kill me?" he asked, trying to keep up with the twists and turns of the last forty seconds. "You're the hitman? Hitperson?" *Who knocked for entry?* he added silently.

"Me? Do wet work?" She threw her head back and pealed laughter at the ceiling. She had, he noticed admiringly, a great laugh. Her hair was plaited in a long blond braid that reached halfway down her back. He wondered what it would look like unbound and spread across his pillow. "Oh, that's very funny, Dr. Dean."

"Thanks, I've got a million of 'em." Pause. "How did you know my name?"

She smiled. It was a nice smile, warm, with no condescension. "It wasn't hard to find out."

"What's *your* name?" he asked boldly. He should have been nervous about the locked door, about the threat to his life. He wasn't. Instead, he was delighted at the chance to talk to her, after a day of thinking about her and wondering how she was—*who* she was.

"Kara."

"That's gorgeous," he informed her, "and I, of course, am not surprised. You're so pretty! And so deadly," he added with relish, "you're like one of those flowers that people can't resist picking and then—bam! Big-time rash."

"Thanks," she said. "I think." She blushed, which gave her high color and made her eyes bluer. He stared, besotted. He didn't think women blushed anymore. He didn't think women who beat up thugs blushed at all. He was very much afraid his mouth was hanging open, and he was unable to do a thing about it. "Dr. Dean—"

"Umm?"

"—I'm not sure you understand the seriousness of the situation."

"Long, tall, and ugly is out to get me," he said, sitting down opposite her. He shoved a pile of charts aside; several clattered to the floor and she watched them fall, amused. "But since you're not the hitman, I'm not too worried."

"Actually, I'm your self-appointed bodyguard."

"Oh, well, then I'm not worried at all," he said with feigned carelessness, while his brain chewed that one—*bodyguard?*—over.

GREAT BOOKS,
GREAT SAVINGS!

When You Visit Our Website:
www.kensingtonbooks.com

You Can Save Money Off The Retail Price
Of Any Book You Purchase!

- **All Your Favorite Kensington Authors**
- **New Releases & Timeless Classics**
- **Overnight Shipping Available**
- **eBooks Available For Many Titles**
- **All Major Credit Cards Accepted**

Visit Us Today To Start Saving!
www.kensingtonbooks.com

All Orders Are Subject To Availability.
Shipping and Handling Charges Apply.
Offers and Prices Subject To Change Without Notice

Contemporary Romance by

Kasey Michaels

Say Yes! to Sizzling Romance by
Lori Foster